YOU

Chronicles of a Stalker with ADD

a novel

with

The Ill-usives

street fiction

by

mark damon puckett

ONION SCRIBE PUBLISHING

ALSO BY MARK DAMON PUCKETT

The Reclusives

CONTENTS

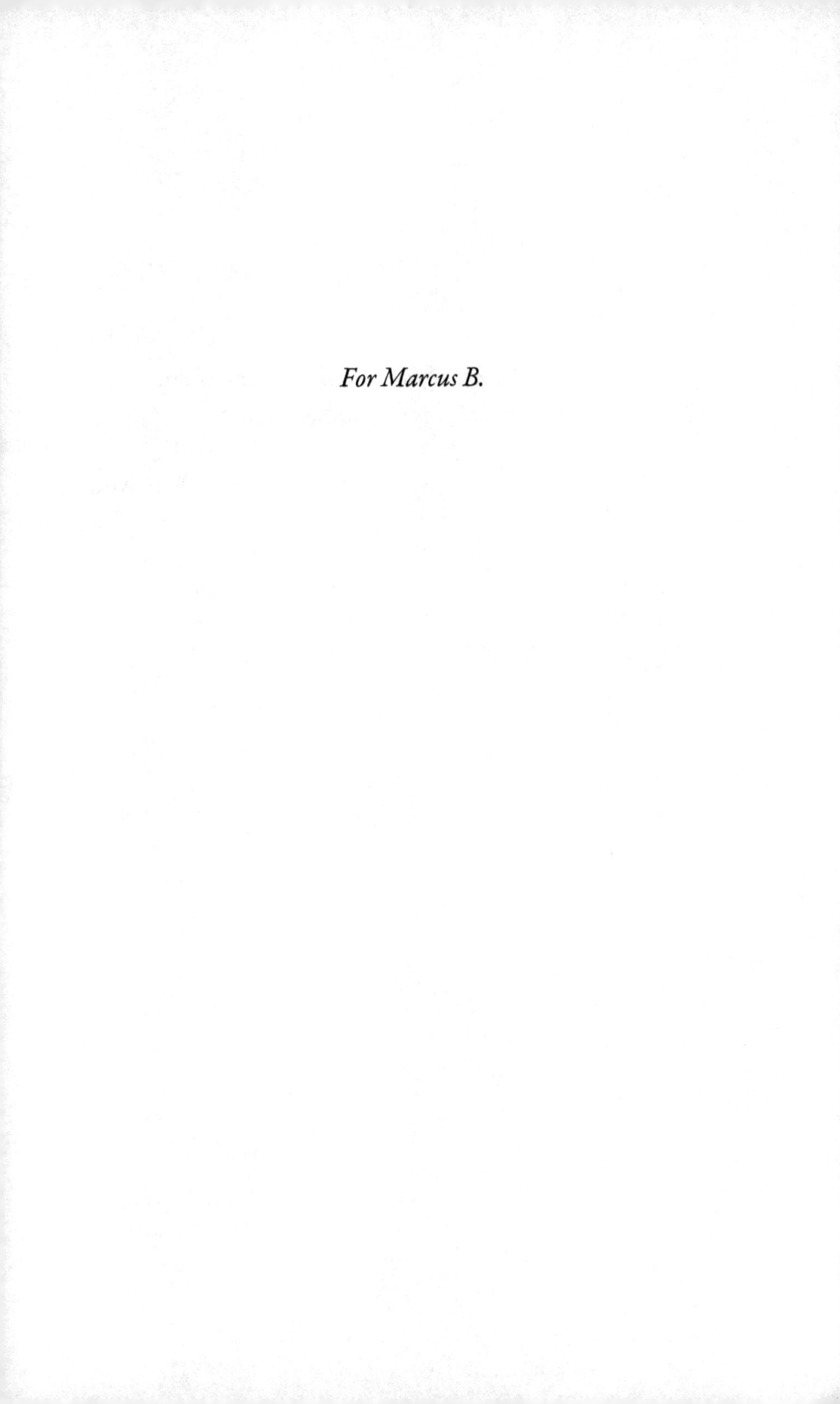

For Marcus B.

. . . All is not right in his head, but he lives.
And that is something, is it not?

—Paul Auster,
City of Glass

STALKING TRAINING

9:15 a.m.

Here at Stalking Training, you will learn the algorithms of how to become a good stalker. Your applications were screened and the final pool of ten was based on the survey you completed. In your answers, you listed the specificities of how you are fed up with stupid people, commonly known as the booboisie. You are here because, through this survey, you let us know that you believe the following:

SOME PEOPLE SHOULD BE STALKED, BUT SOME PEOPLE SHOULD BE MORE STALKED THAN OTHERS

Now, a few of you claim actual experience, as stalkers, and are already fixated on a person whom you may or may not have followed at some point. Let's get something straight. You are no more than epigone amateurs with factitious aptitude if you think "innate talent" can qualify you to stalk. Anybody can follow anybody. But to truly stalk—this involves finesse and critical yet subtle attention to nuance.

Not to say that some of you don't have a natural prowess; if you didn't, you wouldn't be here. But do not become overconfident about this flea of ability. You are here to learn how to scare and annoy people in a calculated, elegant way.

We don't hate our victims. We merely want to teach them about themselves. They are the litterers, the nasty neighbors, the scoffers of children, the entitled golfers, the women with overbaked plastic surgery, the slow people in minivans in the left lane, the loud men in suits on cell phones talking about "the market", the teenage girls who say "like" every other word, the "actors" on reality television.

In other words: the unconscious.

*See, we are the conscious. We are aware of things they are not because we are tuned in to the small thing. They are the people without superegos. No one has ever told them to stop being so noisy on their phones. And if they **have** been told, they haven't heard it. As a result they have gotten away with this all their lives, which means that we are the extreme to balance out their lack of compunction.*

Any questions so far . . . ?

What if I don't have a stalking victim yet?
Ah, good one.

Well, once you pay your fee and officially enroll today, that won't be a problem. First, we will inventory your personal life for any potential enemies. Bad neighbors are fantastic candidates, but there is not a lot of distance between your house and a neighbor's, leaving very little room to actually stalk. So we suggest, in this case, that you fixate for a while on, perhaps, a film icon, then we shall end up using that symbology to transfer it over to someone more locally stalkable.

I don't think I have that natural gift you mentioned. Do I still have a chance to be a good stalker?
Hey, these are really great questions.

*Let me tell you a story. I've stalked about ten people in my life, two currently, and I've never been caught **and** I have no restraining orders. I even stalked a family member. Immediate family!*

[Light applause.]

Here is the secret and really the first lesson. You need to broaden your vision to multiple people, not just one. The best stalkers can multi-stalk. For example, and this is the story I want to relay, one of my two current stalkees is an ex-boyfriend. He and I had our troubles, sure, but my reason for coming after him, for crippling his quotidian habits and for always making him look over his shoulder, is that I deeply love him. I feel it is necessary for him to pay mind to the reminders. I am, in essence, a corporeal reminder. I am also proof that a woman can be a stalker as well.

I thought this was for rapists.

Whoa! Stalkers and rapists are two whole different wax balls. Let's not get ahead of ourselves. Please, let's take this offline, you and I, so I can get back on message.

Okay, if there are no more preliminary questions, then I think we should get all your paperwork completed. There are administrative aides here with your folders and you will work with them, get them your $500 checks and sign all your waivers.

I, if you can believe it, need to go stalk my ex-boyfriend, so I will see you back here at 10:30 a.m. This is also your last chance to drop the course. Bear in mind though that you have been meticulously screened. Chosen as prophets, of a sort. We feel you are the best new ethicists for teaching propriety to fractious idiots.

Once you have signed everything and become "official", the real work will commence.

See you in about an hour.

10:30 a.m.

Welcome back! I've heard from my admins (one of whom I'm stalking (more of a "practice" thing)) that everyone has paid and accepted the gauntlet. No one has dropped. I am very happy about 100% participation.

[Multiple gunshots from several guns are heard.]

Wait! Keep your seats, keep your seats. We knew this might happen, having the seminar at the shooting range. They are doing their best to keep the gun lanes next to us empty during our time here, but there are still members who will be coming and going to shoot. Relax. And face it, sometimes stalkers might need a gun for "effect". Although we never encourage anyone to kill another person, we hold the session at this place in the event that you might like to a) buy a gun, b) practice using it, c) take the gun seminar at this location.

For the moment, look around you. You will see that of the ten candidates here, including myself as the eleventh, your leader, we all have a diverse mix of races and genders. We do not screen on gender or race, merely on your answers that we blindly judge without knowledge of what you look like. It just so happens, however, that half of you are men and half women. This accidental symmetry proves that there is a universal order to things. Some of you are hispanic, white, african, indian, chinese. We have an assorted group here, proving even further that stalking is completely democratic. We are, indeed, ecumenical.

However, we caution you to never stalk for revenge, for it will lead you to a very disturbing internal place. There is an inherent concinnity in pursuing someone as a profession and therein knowing that stalking can be a structured art. This is really the essence of what you will learn in our seminar that other stalking seminars do not provide. While the seminar lasts six months and you keep a journal during that time, you will spend another six months continuing the journal into your first stalking experiences.

*To demonstrate how **not** to stalk, there is a case study we have published by one of our former clients, and we want you to read and discuss it first. This client attended our very seminar many years ago, his journal later popularized. In his particular situation there was also the issue of an attention deficit disorder, keeping him from zeroing on his subjects with any focused acuity. Now, earlier, I did mention multi-stalking as acceptable, even encouraged. In his sad case, though, he found himself stalking a person but, because he was a writer, ended up losing sight of the victim and stalking things like words. Or the sun. Or God. And if I'm not mistaken, I think he even stalked himself once! It's hard to know what's true in his case because there is too much confabulation, but as we read it together, we can examine his failure as a stalker of people and how it helps us to avoid self-aggrandizing hazards of our own. Stalking, in the end, is about others.*

We will now break into groups to discuss the case study entitled, YOU. *On the one hand, we can read it as the memoir of a failed* stalker **or** we can look at it as a logophile offering us a personal exegesis of his love of language.

[More gunshots.]

There is definite stalking in this confessional but a different method altogether, which has caused an ongoing controversy in our circles. For example, some extremist stalking trainers use YOU as a cult pedagogy. In other words, just as we employ it as a cautionary case study today, others are lauding it as the raw truth of stalking and teaching it as a bible. Their argument is that you can stalk words or the sun or yourself just as much as you can people. For our purposes, we present it to you to fulfill our ethos that only people are worth stalking, not words. And certainly not God. Thank you.

[More gunshots.]

Enjoy the seminar. And never forget our credo: "Always stalk on every walk."

YEAH, YOU

More than likely you have seen me elsewhere but have ignored me or reacted in a horrified, supercilious—hey, shut up, let me finish—manner to my face, due to the fact that my eyes are crossed.

Nevertheless, I see straight. And I remember *your* eyes.

But you are drawn to me like a kamikaze moth. Full of cutting judgment too. You whisper to yourself after I pass, thinking I am too ignorant to be conscious of your redounding gossip, your miasmic invective. Believe that I know you. I also have good hearing and am aware that you have relegated me to opprobrium.

You watched me yesterday at the magazine rack at Book 'Em, which has a newsstand on the outside and a bookstore on the inside. I planned to buy the literary journal I was reading—not that it's any of your business. You, however, having nothing to do with the newsstand, mumbled something to the clerk who then expropriated it from me, irrupting into my personal space and yanking it from my hands with a venal smirk.

Did you feel better, even though you were perusing a porno magazine with, I believe, no intention of payment? I stared at you briefly and gave you the stinkeye. You, you quisling, would not look me in the walleye. I continued to stare. As you strutted off, your rancid cigar followed you like a lip-cancer ghoul. You, like the clerk, also had a venal smirk. What was this: Venal Smirk Day?

I followed you.

Close behind.

All day I was your shadow. I have a car, as you discovered, which is not mine. Periodically, I hijack a vehicle but still like to call it my own, inasmuch as I took the time out of my busy day to steal it. I jotted down your license plate, just in case I lost you. I never did. I kept you in my sight. You glanced in your rearview mirror often. What have I done, you must have asked yourself, screeching onto this side street or that alley in order to lose me. You had been petty. You knew your actions were—do not interrupt me—ignoble.

You drove around the city through the purple hills, the neon, the sybaritic neighborhoods, the squalor on the outskirts. Palm trees quivered like the legs of a newborn fawn. Nice simile? Yes, I know. I happen to love words more than people. And I happen to love similes more than parties (which typically contain multiple people and rarely any decent similes).

I wondered what had merited your incursion into my life? Believe it or not, I had written the story I happened to be reading and was about to buy the literary journal. But you prevented me from purchasing that last copy. I had searched all day for it, stopping at four newsstands. The magazine with my story does not print in large numbers. And they pay very little, sometimes nothing. Most literary writers like myself die friendless in the septic gutter with intoxicated livers, noxious underarms and no life insurance. Many are persistent masturbators. We need all the help we can get.

In fact, by the time I steal a car, use up a day's worth of gas and buy my own literary journal (since they don't give me a free copy), I sink deeper into a personal financial deficit. Let's not forget the $500 I had to fork out for stalking training.

I had *almost* decided to leave you alone, to return to my telephoneless apartment of one room, to forget about you. But then you had to go and pull over your car at a gas station on Sunset near that blue church with all the scientologists. You pointed at me, gesticulating with your eyes wide. This further blame was more than I could tolerate. Luckily, the man to whom you spoke saw no harm and shrugged and thought you were insane. I waved to him. Now you understand how *I* feel. Seeing that the attendant who pumped your gas was indifferent to your whining, you made the decision to confront me. You glanced from side to side as you came my way.

Leave me alone, you entreated. Please.

I wanted to study you. Why had you bothered me? I had done nothing to you.

Please stop, you said. I have a family.

You gazed at my crossed eyes, trying to assess which one worked, which one did not. I crossed them a bit more to make it more difficult for you.

I beg you, you repeated.

Tilting my head, I gazed at your corpulent neck, your folds of bread dough skin, your three chins and assumed you had a trencherman's appetite. You looked like a statue I had once seen of Gluttony. You had certainly taken embonpoint to the next porcine level. For someone like myself who starved all the time, I was intrigued with fat. I reached over to touch you, but it was not as you thought. I wanted to grasp a large piece of your flesh to see what it felt like. Reacting like a hissing opossum in the bottom of public trash can, you held up your two palms as if they could stop me.

Did I have a gun? A knife?

You struggled furiously to waddle back into your car. The funny thing is that I never showed you my weapon. You just knew. And with this, I balled up your license number and decided to leave you.

After, however, a little lesson.

Leaving my stolen car at the gas station, I opened your passenger door, pointed my blade tip on your bulging carotid artery and told you to drive to this very alley, where we have been for the last twenty minutes during my one-on-one lecture. I learned about the one-on-one lecture in stalking training. The rest of the seminar was not very useful. You couldn't concentrate because of all the gun shots.

Now, I informed you, that's the last of the lecture. I will go away on one condition.

Anything! Just stop talking.

Translate annuit coeptis for me.

What? you gasped so stertorously that I thought you were snoring and choking at the same time.

Come on, three seconds. One Mississippi, two Mississ—

Okay okay, you tried, annuit means . . . year?

Loud-buzzer-wrong-sound! Everybody thinks that. Annuit coeptis means *God favors our undertakings.* One more chance: what is a Canopic jar?

I-I don't know. More of your gasping.

Hey sir? Sir? Don't faint. Aw, come on. A Canopic jar holds the entrails of an embalmed body. In Egypt, of course. No, wait, I'm not going to embalm you. Sir? Hey. You there? Oops.

At home: guilt. I shouldn't have threatened you. It was not my place to scare you and cause you to pass out. They warned us about this in the seminar. First, let me say I am sorry. I have low blood sugar. If I don't eat enough protein, I fill with spite at the slightest irking and become tetchy and atrabilious.

Nothing prepared me for today, though, because I assumed my diet was fine. Unfortunately, the Los Angeles sun was too hot. Dehydration burned into my eyes as I craved water. And all the driving to find my little story led only to disappointment. Thanks to you.

You can rest easy tonight, at least. I might even look for you tomorrow to apologize face-to-face. To atone for my error, I would love to make it up to you. Over a cup of chai tea? I *love* chai tea because it has a redivivus effect on my posture.

We'll see. I have a busy schedule. Just kidding. I do nothing all day but bother people. Still, I don't know if I like you. Do *not* cross my path again, all right? At least for a little while until I sort out how I feel about the whole thing. I hope you're not still passed out and/or dying in the alley. That's my bad.

A preprandial gin donated from my neighbor and a good evening meal of seven almonds sent me into a pleasant repose. The following morning I stretched my arms and touched the gray wall next to me, cool as toilet porcelain. I have no windows. An idea struck me. I would go back to the newsstand and still buy my story. Since I had worn my clothes to bed, all I needed to do was splash water on my face and clean the blood from my chin (not sure how it got there). But the landlord had turned off my water. Again.

Halfway to the newsstand, I smacked my head. I had forgotten to eat. Oh well. I didn't have any food, so what was la difference? Habit reminded me I should eat; reality let me know that the habit was just left over from a previous time when meals were consistent.

I parked on the street, a different car (red, sports) than yesterday (white, station wagon), and walked to the newsstand.

Surely, no one would have bought my story—I mean to say, the *magazine* containing my story.

The editor had liked my piece a lot. He had found a little extra money in his funds for me, a check I was supposed to be receiving that had not yet arrived. Turns out, he was a writer like me once until he knocked up somebody. He said he didn't write anymore— something about his wife (the one he knocked up) making it just about impossible for him to concentrate and also censoring most of his creative thoughts, due to the fact that she knew he didn't love her. But he sure enjoyed being an editor with a paycheck, he claimed, despite his viragoish wife's endless objurgating and billingsgate comingled with the poo-changing of butt bisque from an unwanted baby. I could hear her cursing him in the background as we spoke on the phone. He added: I also don't miss starving.

Everybody misses starving, I thought, although I knew he wouldn't understand. We start off starving; it's the first thing we babies know. T.S. Eliot said, "Most editors are failed writers, then again so are most writers." Writing is no life for anyone, nor is stalking for that matter. At least I'm not a flaneur. Stalkers have algorithmic goals. Flaneurs, psh, whatever. Drips.

At the rack, wait, where was my story? It was gone. You! Your improvidence had now deprived me, twice.

There was a different clerk at the cash register.

Excusé the moi? I tossed out some street French casually.

He looked at me askance.

Did I seem so strange?

Why did he stare?

Do you have such and such magazine? I asked him, with the decorum of a grandmother searching for the address to a quilting bee.

Sold the last copy this morning, he grunted. He looked like a gnu with some sort of permutation of a goatee that might also have been a facial brilloesque pad. I could see tomato paste flecks dotting the hair on this hirsute aberration, probably left over from some cheap lunch spot where pasta was a dollar and came with a generic cola.

The rest of the day I searched frantically for a remaining copy. My stomach hurt and I passed out once while driving, screeching all over creation (if the sidewalk can be considered creation). No traffic was near. God is on my side, I thought, as I backed away from the bashed post office box. I prayed a little and noticed a movie poster at a nearby bus stop. Suddenly, Jim Carrey said something to me. I could have sworn it was a joke. "Guy walks into his psychiatrist's office, says, 'I think I'm shrinking.' Psychiatrist says, 'Well, you have to be a little patient.'"

What? I said. *What*?

But he was just kidding, saying nothing at all but acting like he was. Jiiiim.

I found a pay phone, parked the car and waited for a woman to finish, giving her some stranger-danger attitude to quicken her pace. She dropped the receiver and ran, the phone dangling from the metal cord like hanged cat. I know I'm painfully attractive, though, and she didn't faze me. She was probably a street person while I, I am up there with model material.

I slid a quarter into the slot. It fell. I dialed. Sliding quarters into a slot was a quasi-erotic experience.

Hello, may I speak to the editor?

This's he.

I told him about my attenuated cash situation, as in I had none.

That was our last issue. We're defunct. Ran out of money.

No copies left? What happened to the audience?

I have to go, he said. We never had an audience. I'm also getting a divorce. He hung up.

What can I do about my story? I should have made a copy when I wrote it. How sad. Copies are cheap these days and I still couldn't afford them. I am hesitant to ever blame someone for my problems, but had it not been for you yesterday, I would have the magazine right now. I am coming after **you** to let you know what you have done.

Do you know what it is like to see your words on the page of a magazine? You want to share it with your neighbors. But these "people" around you don't care and think that you're pompous if you show off your publication to them. I know them. They try so hard to not be impressed as they misprize you, belittle you with silence. All you want for them to say is, *You must be proud.*

Now I will find you.

The first step was to wait like an orange kitten about to pounce on a grasshopper. I parked on Sunset. On occasion, I walked up the hill to Spago where I was shunned for micturating in the women's restroom without being a patron. Or I crossed the street to look at

Wayne Newton cd's at Tower Records to scrutinize them for any evidence that he was the apperceived second coming. Once, I bought an onion sandwich at Subway. Yes, I mostly eat onion sandwiches. It is my gustatory favorite. Imagine my astonishment when Wayne Newton came into Subway. And you know what they say: once you see *one* star, you are bound to see a litany of them. As soon as I came back to the newsstand, they were all over the galaxy.

Johnny Depp came into the newsstand and bought lots of magazines with Kate Moss on the covers. I'm dating myself here because he dated Kate Moss so long ago. In the end, we all date ourselves. I watched him. He raised his eyebrows at me, indicating a camaraderie of sorts.

Fabio read a magazine called *Video Toaster*. I didn't talk to him. I think it is very hard to be Fabio in a non-Fabio world.

At a certain point, it was too stifling and warm outside at the newsstand and I went inside to read books and feel air conditioning.

I saw Meg Ryan buy some children's books. She sneezed and I said, *Bless you.* It was like I was meant to be there to say it. She giggled back a thank you. She wanted me, but I was not in the mood.

Donald Sutherland bought about thirty Penguin Classics of the Greek wars. He smiled at me when I picked up one of the books he dropped.

Whoopi Goldberg had a problem finding the theater section. I directed her there. I was not in the mood when she, also, wanted me.

I got into a conversation with Robert Downey, Jr., and even though I wasn't an employee, I sold him a large dictionary.

No sign of you, however. Where *were* you? Why should I spend my time thinking of you? Pfft. I cared nothing about your life. Hey, wait, I needed to use the time to find my short story. You may think all of my words are in my head, but I forgot the whole thing—that's why I had to see it. To remember. I have a short attention span and can't recall, for the life of me, what I wrote. It will come back to me; it's in there somewhere. Thank goodness I only write short stories. Imagine a novel. I couldn't remember a novel if I tried.

You should have never prevented me from buying my own story. It's humiliating enough to have to purchase the magazine containing your writing, much less have to chase down somebody because he (you) had you (me) kicked out of a book store. For this reason, I will hound you. I graduated stalking training with honors.

I noticed your thin calves and red velour mini-skirt.

You're Kit Fisher. I read your story. You're Kit Fisher! you repeated, incredulous upon meeting an obscure person like myself.

Tsk, I thought, typical literary journal groupie. I could see them coming a mile off. But there is only like, well, one, and I had always wanted to meet her (you).

You sat in my car and removed your short skirt to reveal nothing underneath. Then you forced me to lap the moist hair between your legs, actually holding my head there while exclaiming, I'm your bitch in heat. I had not expected this canine role-playing and developed chin chafe.

You were good to me except for the occasional sado-masochism. Alas, our schedules ended up being too different. I sleep during the day and write during the night and stalk when the mood hits. You liked this part of me initially (the first hour), until, that is, you began referring to me as a vampiric incubus.

Your idiosyncrasies were manifold. I can't even count them now. I didn't love you. You were messy. To make matters worse, you thought I was messy. We blamed each other for our messiness. I soon grew tired of you calling me Wittle Doggie.

And does it *really* matter if I have murdered? We all have ghosts under our beds. If I tell you that I have, you will judge me. Since you have already sentenced me anyway, I don't need that—even if I wasn't a killer but decided to tell you I was just for a joke. I know what murder is, though. I see myself in the act often. To be honest, I could never kill anyone. But make them suffer: by all means.

I'll tell you something, if you promise to refrain from assuming I am guilty. I do, as you guessed before, have a knife. A mediumish one. I sharpen it whenever I can and wear it on my side, which may account for some leers I receive. Because I am so sensitive about the personal area around me, those few inches that allow us freedom in ourselves, I can't allow anyone to trespass this sanctified area. If you do, I won't kill you, but I will draw blood. I know how.

May we have sex again? Ah, good. Very good. Ooo. Nice. No fetching this time. Please may I have a treat?

After sex, I told you about my life. You begged me for a story. Once, I was at LAX, parked in a lane with no cars. As you know, you can't dawdle at the airport or you will be towed immediately. Well, not me. I found a space away from the flux and remained there, waiting for a friend who asked me pick him up. Keep in mind, please, that I was hurting no one and blocking no traffic.

Suddenly, I glanced in my mirror and saw him: a man with white hair in a truck. He honked his horn like a goose maniac. I ignored him. What was his problem? He beeped again louder and longer.

Sighing, I shook my head. Did I do something bad? Did I deserve this extraneous noise?

I'd like to say the matter ended here. Unfortunately, he drove into me, bumping me and pushing me forward. I pressed the brake, but my stolen car, in park, still moved. His truck was giant.

That's *it*, I thought. I opened my door (the car still being pushed), walked to him and leaned my head in his window.

The coward stared ahead, as if he didn't see me.

Excuse me, but is this necessary?

He remained staring ahead with the vacantly hostile eyes of an owl in a barn. Planes made unreasonable racket around us and the area smelled of warm oil fumes.

Car's in the way, he grunted, rolling his tongue around his mouth in a bored manner.

I'm going to stab you in the face, I warned him as I walked beside the slowly moving truck still nudging my car along.

Yeah, he snorted with laughter, you couldn't stab a piece of watermelon with a fork.

With my left hand fingers I pinched his cheek between the upper and lower jaw, grabbing quite a bit of skin. He slapped at my wrist and finally stopped his truck. Wielding my knife with my right hand, I stabbed him through the cheek and pulled the blade out quickly. After it was done, I grabbed his collar and yanked him toward me. Did I slice his throat? Of course not. But he had dented my bumper (or whoever's car it happened to be). I gave him what he deserved.

Most people would accept such behavior. Not I. I'm a walking superego. NB: I am not a psychopath. I just want people to know what is wrong and what is right. What he did was not right. If you stab someone in the cheek, it takes a long time to heal. I envisioned a small homeless bug crawling in the hole at night for a place to rest on his tongue. Think of it in this way: whenever his tongue gropes for that sore, he is sure to remember his error. And me. Plus the fat knife in his face. To be a good teacher, you have to take the time.

I'm just a writer, though, because I'm too afraid to be a criminal. My point is that the stabbing of the gent was better than the act of writing. If I write a novel and you read it, you might be changed from your previous state to something better. Fiction can help. Like my short story you read. Now, a wound is a *real* reminder. A wound is a better artifice than a story. A story may exist forever, yet it is dormant until acted upon by the reader. A wound is always active. Just think about when you see a woman whose flesh remains burned, even long after it has healed. Same goes for having crossed eyes. Once you are marked, in any way, you will never forget your wound. I did the right thing and you can't convince me otherwise. A story just doesn't do the trick anymore. I justify war for these very reasons.

Suddenly, you stood from the bed, put on your mini-skirt and accused me of having an evil core. Describing me as dangerous and vulnerable, an impossible integration, you asked me to leave. I had only been with you and your thin calves for two hours. You asked me not to return. Seeing me at the door, your eyes belied this request.

YOU AGAIN

Seems a plane had crashed or so said the headlines of the newspaper through the dispenser. I used to feel respect for the dead (*de mortuis nil nisi bonom*), but since there are too many folks in the world, I tend to breathe a sigh of relief when mass deaths occur. More oxygen for me.

Let's face it about the world population. The food will run out soon. Maybe the Muslims and Mormons could get into a war and annihilate each other? We have no good wars anymore. It used to be that when people got too hostile, they had an old-fashioned World War that killed about fifty million. Nowadays, nobody has the time. We end up just murdering each other in traffic. If the Baptists killed the Catholics, the Episcopalians killed the Jehovah's Witnesses, and so on, we could effectively wipe out religion. Then all the politicians could declare war on the bankers. Oh, and finally strippers would kill all the actors. War would certainly wipe out the need for writing and stalking.

By the way, I have given up my search for you. It is not right to blame you for what happened. I thought about something: what if that plane crash had occurred at the newsstand and burnt my magazine story? Would I then pursue the pilot for his errant driving? Or blitzkrieg the air traffic controller who was responsible? Of course not. So why blame you? You thought I was a miscreant at a newsstand. As I see it, you wanted to do a decent deed. How can I see you as anything but a good man?

I'll tell you how, you coward! If you are amiable to me, I reciprocate this good cheer. Otherwise, I have to stamp out inequity. I am no superhero. Just a person who believes the elite mistakenly sees the proletariat as lower than itself. Yet, as we all know, no human being is under another. This is not India! I am using too many exclamation points! When I was a kid, I thought they were "explanation" points!

I cannot seem to focus on anything with a good thesis statement. I could never figure out the thesis statement during my studies, but apparently it is very important in colleges, universities and Nazism. I wish there was a drug for people with short attention spans. I can't believe that the pharmaceuticals have not come up with that one yet. Maybe, while they're at it, they can also come with a drug for helping with thesis statements.

Look, I'll spare you my opinions; you need to get your own. How do you get your own opinions, you ask? Well, you can't. Firstly, your parents formed you. Then all of your teachers and friends. Then all the books you read. You have no opinions that are not an evolution of derivative thought. Even your feelings are not your own. But we have invented language which allows us to, more than anything else, lie to ourselves that we are unique. We are not. We are chemical chunkules of skin with simian brains and we have copied every damn thing we know and do. Some are just better copiers than others.

Unfortunately, my brain malady allows me to be different from the rest of you apish automatons. All of my thoughts are not lies, like yours. Mine are original. I have perception and it is a sickness. If I were not sick, I would think just like you. My sickness is perception; therefore, I see.

Ah! An idea occurs. I will ask the man at the newsstand who you are, your identity. He'll know because you are a regular porn customer. But it will require a disguise.

He recognized me in three seconds.

Who was that man yesterday? I asked, referring to you.

I don't know what you're talking about.

But—

Why are you wearing a dress?

He is a friend. (In a way, I do consider you my best friend from all the time we have spent together.)

I gave him five dollars.

His large eyes darted from left to right then back to me.

Okay, he muttered, come on Wednesday. He'll be here around ten o'clock to buy his weekly porn.

He = you.

Four nights until Wednesday. No food. No money. I plan to take yours if you don't offer me a meal. I've got it! I will try to remember what I wrote. I will write my story again. After all, it was only four pages. I've forgotten every word.

I missed your thin calves and returned to you. Against your will, you invited me to your warm bed, never questioning me about the red dress I wore. After simulating puppy sex, we discussed sin. I stay away from big vices like rape and murder; a *little* theft here and there is good for the soul. Once, I robbed a policeman. I know he serves and protects, but he harassed me for no reason, something about my knife and a yellow sun dress I sometimes wear. I think he even poked fun of my make-up which was like a Christmas tree all across my face. In order to be safe I have vowed to be quick, so when the first words came from his mouth (whispering to himself, Faggot), I stepped on his toe with my heel and stabbed him in the cheek, which, as you can now guess, is my trademark contusion.

Did I react too quickly?

What undoes prejudice? A simple prestidigitation? Wave the hand and, poof, his bigotry vanishes?

No. Even if he changed, what anodyne could have the efficacy to allow me to recover from his insult? I don't like names. You never forget them. Of course I was in horror a second later. Given that I had stolen the policeman's wallet, I wondered what sort of reprobate I really was. Deep down, you know? Faggot was just a name. Hell, in the fourth grade, if another kid called me a faggot and I tattled and the teacher scolded him, he usually said, "I only meant to call him 'a bundle of sticks.'"

If I helped the policeman after stabbing and robbing him, he was sure to come after me later. I don't like jail. Those convicts in the hoosegow are very bitter. Either that, or they are reborn, and you know how that can be. Why does everyone "find" Jesus there? Who lost him? Stop losing Jesus! For that matter, stop finding him!

My apartment, where I write, is like a cell. I don't mind. It offers the semblance of jail and that is not so bad; in fact, feeling like you are in jail without actually having to be there can really make you appreciate where you are: safe at home and not having your anus probed by a convicted rapist who justifies his behavior with specific biblical passages.

You stared at me. Perhaps it was gawking. You were a good listener. You were my temporary girlfriend.

The people who hurt my feelings don't die; I just wound them. Don't call me a vigilante. I'm not one of those at all. I am the Onion Scribe who peels away the layers of falsehood, forcing the world into involuntary tears as it views the truth.

The Onion Scribe? Who's that?

I am the Onion Scribe, I repeated.

You stared at me: I'm not just a groupie like you wrote about me in your journal.

You read my personal journal? Don't do that.

Hey, I'm the only one who read your story, remember?

Seriously, those are my private thoughts.

But you had fallen asleep. So sweet you looked.

I left.

Four nights to wait.

YOUR BEER IS IN A BAG

At the bus stop you offered me a sip from your beer can in a paper bag. Boy, your breath needs work. Pee-ew. Do you brush your tongue? They say tongue brushing prevents halitosis. No doubt I will have insomnia tonight—no doubt about it. Here's what happens to me. I will read a long time. My eyes never tire. Then I will write a story that is just whatever I have read filtered through mesh. The question is: which is my story: the stuff on top of the mesh or the stuff that passes through?

I think with my eyes open in the dark and I listen to the silence and wonder how it is much louder than any noise. I cannot sleep. When I do (and it is only when exhaustion descends like a hammer on a nail), I cannot rouse myself. I am unable to wake because I refuse to dream, and when I refuse to dream, I sleep until I do. And I do dream. If I sleep twenty hours, which is pretty normal for me, then through some strange balancing property, I remain awake for this exact amount of time.

Thank you for your indulgence and listening about my writing process. I can no longer tolerate your breath. No, I do not have an extra bus token. I also do not want a handjob.

I nearly forgot you.

How do you elude me, then, all of a sudden appear to me?

Do I choose to forget you?

If so, why does your image recur? Hm? Any answers?

You are my thesis statement, I think.

I vacillate in my opinions of you. More often than not, I view you as insignificant, a body of trivial veins and irrelevant bones.

All day I couldn't stand you.

First, due to what you had done to me at the magazine rack.

Then, as a result of having to avenge the loss of my story.

Then, guilt for wanting revenge.

Then, anger for feeling guilty.

Then, guilt for the anger.

Then, still not knowing what a thesis statement was.

And so forth.

As you see, you waste my time. Half of my day is squandered. By the time I write down these thoughts, the stars begin to pepper the sky like salt. Or simply salt the dark sky. Stars don't look like pepper, I just realized. They look more like salt. I love to lick salt sometimes. People who invented salt shakers must make *bank*. I know the chemical formula for salt is NaCl. In high school I mispronounced this as Nackle for a few days and went around saying, "Pass the Nackle," when I meant, "Pass the salt." One day a bully corrected me. Before he punched my face, he added, "I'm surprised you don't get beat up more often."

Do you know that I never take a vacation? When I finish one book, I pick up another, sometimes reading three to ten of them at once. Why? I have no friends, for one. I'm devoted to a life you don't understand.

Take my schedule, for instance. I wake at a different time every day. Notice I did not say every morning, for I try to avoid this time. Morning. It's homonymic connection to "mourning" cannot be an accident.

On the rarest occasion, morning is fine. The other day, before we met, I walked up Hauser with a basketball I had stolen from a sporting goods store. I bounced the ball as I trotted along, listening to the morning birds and smelling the sweet flora before car exhaust consumed the air. We live in a big city with many cars, don't we?

Around six a.m., if you find the right neighborhood, you can feel the cool and breathe in the oxygen of hibiscus and pretend to smell the bougainvillea that has no smell. I always check. Why not? They are flowers, aren't they? Whoever heard of a flower with no smell, especially one with such a long french name? Beautiful flowers without smell must indicate something about the city that produces them.

I dribbled the ball on the sidewalk. No cars anywhere. Quite a relief in a section normally filled with deafening vehicles. An older chinese man stooped to pick up an aluminum can in his yard. After he stood, he remained stooped. Maybe he had osteoporosis. If that's what happens to me when I'm old, please set me in front of an archery target and send one arrow through my forehead and one into my heart.

Have you heard what happens when you get old? First of all, you never sleep. You sit in bed with your eyes wide open. You have no appetite. You lose your teeth. Oh, if you don't detect your gingivitis early, you can't get dentures. You have to gum everything. And do you know what everything is? How about a nice bowl of applesauce? Mm, mm. That's breakfast. For lunch, guess what? A bowl of mashed up black-eyed peas. Or lima beans. Or pork and beans. But mashed. You can be sure of that. Don't forget your dinner of a mashed potato.

Therefore, you can look forward to osteoporosis, mashed food and, if you're lucky, you won't have anybody who loves you, plus you'll likely end up slobbering in the booby hatch, a hospital, or a "rest home" full of other zombified elders. You get to listen to them drool. Every day, you can guarantee someone will break his or her hip, but since vocal cords seize up around seventy, no one can discuss these tragedies, save for the voluble exceptions who couldn't shut up if their lives depended on it, which they don't because their lives depend on nothing except having their insurance money and all their assets sucked dry by whoever owns the convalescent home.

Then there's Alzheimer's. I used to have this really great aunt who knelt to my level and sneaked me two dollars and kissed me. She smelled like baby powder and she was the warmest lady I ever knew. She got Alzheimer's. I visited her by myself once. She just sat in a room on a bed with a hose hooked up to her so she could pee and shit. She held this plastic baby and wore an ugly frown. A nurse who had no feelings came in to feed her and treated her like a retarded circus animal. I ran out of there and cried in the long shiny corridor. She used to give me two-dollar bills.

I bounced the ball past the chinese man and wanted to wave, although around here no one says hello to anyone. It's a tacit understanding that we have enough to worry about without having to deal with annoying salutations. So I said nothing. He didn't notice me. His torso was perpendicular to the ground, as if he were doomed to appear in perpetual search of an elusive insect. I crossed 3rd street, normally busy but not now, and made my way to the park.

I needed to take my mind off *you*.

What what? I am not alone this morning. Two nets had been strung across the middle of the basketball court. On each side was a japanese man or woman. The two couples, the four people, swatted their shuttlecocks and shouted things that sounded like, Heeyash!

Goo' morning, one lady said, after finishing a point. She bowed.

The two games proceeded. They left me enough area to sprint around and act like I was a professional. I missed the first seven lay-ups. Each free throw didn't even hit the rim. One shot slammed the backboard with such velocity that it bounced at me and over my head into one of the badminton games.

Sorry, I said.

They all smiled. Nice people. I would never stalk them. You don't need to stalk nice people, only jerks.

I soon warmed up to my old prowess. Memory oiled the rusty spots and I remembered I could be quite good—if I practiced. I started near the basket and moved around the world, ending on the other side.

Then *you* arrived at the bleachers and sat. So many yous in the world; there always seems to be another one of you when you least expect it. Who were you? You were a bit overweight and you moved slowly, breathing heavily once your bottom rested on the metal seat. You nodded to yourself, as if to say, *Is this what it takes for a man of forty just to sit down*?

I felt awful right then. I had such good health yet I complained constantly about my life. Nothing satisfied me. Roll the dice, I thought, and you're me: that breathless guy who can barely sit without the fear of passing out. Roll the dice and I could have been in a war and lost a leg. Roll the dice and I could have been Albert Camus and had my head torn off in a car accident.

I shot for about another half hour and was about to leave, when you pushed yourself up and walked toward me.

One-on-one? you asked.

I nearly hyper-guffawed. Besides being dressed in dungarees and a wool shirt, you wore work boots. I pointed to myself and raised my eyebrows.

Yeah, you.

The japanese couples had finished and smiled to themselves as they removed the nets.

Full court? you added.

Are you kidding? I almost asked, but then agreed to the match.

Shoot the die.

What? I inquired.

The do-or-die.

Oh.

I stood there.

You know what "the die" is?

Sure don't, I admitted.

You shoot the ball from, say, here. If you make it, you go first. If not, I do.

But no one actually dies? Whew. Do you want to change your clothes or something?

Nah, I'm fine.

Missing the do-or-die (awful phraseology), I bounced the ball to you, so you could start the game. I proceeded to score every point in rapid succession. You never tried to catch me. Whenever you got the ball, you dribbled like a six-year-old with rickets. If you shot, which was rare, you bent over with the ball hanging in both hands and flung it through the air. One time, you actually threw it behind yourself and fell over in the process. I helped you up.

Good game, you said, dusting off your hands. You returned to the bleachers for your jacket, nodded goodbye to me and disappeared down a concrete sidewalk in the park. I was alone again. The birds ceased to sing. The japanese were gone. I bounced the ball and an echo followed. Why can't I be like you, I wondered? You'll probably go home to your wife and tell her how well you played. Or maybe you were making fun of me. Surely not. You meant no harm to anyone. I bounced the ball again. Another echo. In a few minutes the park would begin to fill.

At my apartment I fell asleep, not sure for how long. I own no clock. Upon waking, there was light again. Either I had taken a brief kip or slept over twenty-four hours. I decided to ask someone.

Outside in the hallway I knocked on my neighbor's door.

Hey, I said, apologizing, what day is it?

Five in the morning day, is what.

Stop scratching your balls for a second, I wanted to tell him.

It's the weekend, he grunted.

Saturday?

Mm, he affirmed. Or Sunday?

Thanks for mostly nothing.

Slam.

Three men in a small car drove by me as I strolled down the sidewalk and sang in unison, Nice ass, Lumberjack!

Upon finding a vehicle to drive for that day, I had to worry about a parking space which ended up being somewhere in a residential neighborhood. After locking the car, I began strolling to the same book store.

No sign of you.

Since I love songs, one that I had just heard on the radio had stuck in my mind, a nice tune sung by a woman who misses her husband. What makes it unique is that for some reason I think she is in love with a midget. Without really noticing myself, I sang aloud, snapping my fingers and holding my tongue between my lips, occasionally adding the line, "This song is about a mi-i-dget." I even spun around once and became so entranced I didn't even notice a man to my right in the self-help aisle, who, espying me, caused me to stop. How embarrassing. Instead of giggling, he pointed his finger at me and said, You got it, man. Yeah, you got it.

Got what? How long had he been watching me? He didn't scoff. Hm. He was all right, I guess.

I decided to go back home. You clearly weren't coming to the newsstand. Why was I spending my time on you?! Stop wasting my time!

Back at the apartment door I noticed a commotion at the other end of the hall. A young woman with long black hair, dressed in sweat pants and sweat shirt, knocked on someone's door. She waited.

A voice from inside yelled for her to leave. She knocked again.

I turned the key in my bottom lock but jiggled it a few times so I could watch what she was doing. The door in front of her opened.

Hi, she cooed like an orgasming pigeon, I wondered if you could turn your music down.

I don' care.

It's very loud, she pointed out.

I don' care, the short mexican man repeated.

I saw no face, for he remained within his home. I knew, however, a short mexican man lived there because he had once given me a pack of corn tortillas, having bought one too many at the grocery store. I remember because I had eaten them all in about three seconds.

Well, she said, I'll tell our manager Chester then.

Goheed. I don' care. All Chester do is smoke crack.

Look, she began very nicely. Your music is too loud.

Thass okay. Nobody turn down when I ask. So I don' care.

But I never play my music loud.

Oh yeeeesss, yes you do.

Well, why don't you ask me to turn it down?

I ask but don' nobody listen.

You've never even knocked on my door.

I know.

He stepped over the threshold and touched the jamb. She backed up. They both noticed me. My door was unlocked and open. I rushed inside. Perhaps the girl and I—no, silly thought. She requested a simple favor from another person. She begged a kindness; he refused.

You, from the newsstand, are like the non-music-turning-down man. No moral system. No essential compassion. You live outside the purlieus of trust and honesty. I spent all of my life in education of the soul. Books, church, school: all of these things raise me above you. And yet, irony, you have power because you subsist on the anarchy of my edification.

I am a violent pacifist.

I have respect for you, even if you don't for me.

Excuse me . . . I just vomited. I need a mint.

I have even tried to construct a forgiveness for you by imagining you as a person who at one time knew love and simply forgot it. Were you hurt? Did someone mean hurt you? Okay, if they did, I am willing to forgo my revenge. No. No. I rescind the last statement. I don't care if you were hurt. Do you know why? Because you hurt me. You were in pain, yes, but now you've created more anguish. Do you blame the person who hurt you? Good. But he is no excuse. I'm sorry. I'm still coming after you. *Vae victis*. Woe to the vanquished. Also *irae caelestes*. Divine wrath. Watch it when I break out the Latin, my friend.

Now that you know a little about my life, do you have a bit more sympathy? You see how nice I am? I can't stop thinking about you. You've thrown off everything. Until I see you again, I won't rest easy. But all this will make a good story, I think. Maybe I will even pretend to be more upset with you than I really am, in order to keep the story going.

I talk to people and view situations and write about them. That's all.

In fact, I write now.

I write of you.

You cannot tell when I'm writing and when I'm stalking. That's because I can do both at once. Robert Frost said you must have your vocation and avocation. And I decided that my hobby would be stalking words. I open a dictionary and stare at one. Sometimes, you will see me under a neon sign, staring. It's harmless practice, word-staring.

In point of further fact, my wrists ache and I need to give them and my fingers a rest. Also my palms. You would be surprised how much the palms hurt. I have been writing on this journal for stalking training for hours, maybe days.

I know. I'll go into the hallway and buy a soda from the machine. This fifty cents has been burning a hole in my pocket.

I open my door. Walk down the hall. At the end is the machine. I hear steps, thinking they are my own. Someone, I swear, goes into my apartment. I sense the intrusion behind me.

Before I have time to buy a soda, I massage the quarters between my fingers and think to myself. What a ridiculous phrase: "think to myself". Of course I will think to myself. There's no one else to think to!! I start following the word "think" in my head and began to mentally spin in circles. Stop thinking about think, I think.

My thoughts tell me to bust into a sprint. I'm quite a runner. I nearly pass my own door and have to grab the wall to stop myself.

I jump on top of you. Who are you? With a globe of the earth I pummel your face right where the Philippines are. The globe spins.

You know you can't be in my home.

I find my belt and wrap it around your neck and drag you into the hallway, your fingers trying to peel the leather from your neck.

It is times like these that I wish I lived on the top floor and not in the basement because 1) I can find no stairs to throw you down and 2) if there is an earthquake I will be squished.

I drag you up the hall to the soda machine. You try to stand. I trip you. You fall. I nearly throw my shoulder out of socket as your momentum yanks me forward. At the soda machine I drop in the two quarters. The red can falls like a fast dumbwaiter and I open the drink to gulp the fizzy bevvie. I hiccup.

Why are you in my apartment! I yell. You can't come in there. You've broken the rules.

I-I, you beg.

I don't want to hurt you and I don't want you to come again, so I either have to kill you or convince you not to return. Who are you? A burglar? You can't just burgle me.

What of mine is there to steal? A typewriter? A mattress? A wastebasket? A vellum manuscript or two? Now I know. The creditors. Aw, I don't want to kill you, you zit face. You're just a teenager.

You don't want to kill me?

Nah, I know that you just want me to pay my bills. You are a mere emissary for the credit card whores.

I ask you if you would like to cut a deal, huggermugger, just between you and me. "Between you and me" is a prepositional phrase and "you and me" are the objects. That's why you never say "between you and I" because "I" is always a subject, never an object like "me". I hate when people don't contemplate their use of egregious grammar.

You say sure to my deal. You need a few thousand to appease the big men. These are debts I owe too, so I acquiesce.

We decide to rob a bank together, you and I. You have a truck. I have a rope and a hook. We have endured a million lemons; we are about to make a pool of chlorinated lemonade.

We find a cash machine right in the center of the city where you never see policemen and rig up the rope and hook. I give you the signal. You floor it, tires spinning, cash machine flooding from the wall like a dam breaking. An alarm goes brap. Brap. Brap. Brap.

I find the money and pocket my ample bounty. You fill a bag with your share. I am able to pay you off and be way in the black. I unhook the hook, throw the rope in the bed, shake hands with you and tell you I will walk home. The truck tires squeal off.

I mosey around the block for an hour and return to the site where many cops have congregated close to the ATM.

What happened? I ask.

Somebody yanked out the cash machine.

What? Can I give blood or something?

Sir, move along. We don't need any blood.

So *awful*.

Just move along.

Good luck. I hold up my thumb. *Le pouce en l'air*. Then I hold up my other one. Both thumbs are up. *Deux pouces*.

At home I count my money and pay some bills. No more debt. I am free. Owing money no longer saddles me. How should I spend this new lucre? What if someone wants to steal it? I'm being paranoid. No, I'm not. I'm fine. I'm fine. Fine is a polysemous word though. Could be "okay" but could also be a "penalty".

A muffled music pounds through the corridor. Opening my door, I know the mexican man is at it again. I decide to bribe him to stop. No, then he will know I have money. If you flaunt your wealth, it will be stolen from you. Hide the money, Fisher. Get out of the hallway. Protect your investment. The stress! I will give it to charity.

Money dons me with the burden of consciousness and entitlement. I am better than everyone else because I am able to fund whatever I want. One could say that money is simply the codified version of choices. How about offering it to the museum? No, same as giving to the graveyard. Woe is such quickly attained largess. Woe is cash. Only symbolic green paper could plunge me into this much anguish. My debt has been settled. I am flush. Solvency replaces all ratiocination! Before, I was content. I will give it to all the bums or to the church or to an orphanage. What about me though? *Me*. Think of others first, Kit. No. No. If I do, I will be, once again, unable to hold my own. I must think of myself. Whatever's left, I promise to give to a chess club somewhere. Oh let me lose this wad of dough.

You magazine stealer. *You* did this to me. *You* only have a few days.

YOU NEED TO STOP BEING DISTRACTED BY WINDMILLS

Stealing yet another car, I drove on I-10 away from the city to the place in the desert where the Joshua Trees grow. However, I forgot where I was headed and passed right by the exit for highway 62 and ended up in Quartzsite, Arizona. The old car began to splutter in the heat rising from the ground like gas fumes. I pulled in to a garage and a man named Floyd from West Virginia fixed the fuel filter and told me about his (seven) heart attacks. He worked without a shirt, his bypass scars lining his sunburnt chest. I needed to go back to the place in the desert with the Joshua Trees, but Floyd was jactitating about oil and his aorta.

Heading west again I missed the exit again for highway 62 off I-10. I braked the Nova and veered onto the shoulder, where I parked the car and stared at the windmills spinning against the lavender and pink mosaic sky. Cars and trucks whizzed past me, each vehicle causing a coming-to-get-you **whoosh**.

By then it was mid-afternoon, three o'clock. I opened my door. Since part of the vehicle was still on the highway, a tractor trailer honking its horn smashed into the door, yanked it from the hinges and sent it sailing through the air like a punted football. The amputated door landed a few hundred feet ahead in front of a speeding Chevy Citation, which had to stop so abruptly that it caused a nineteen-car collision, traffic thick even ninety miles outside the city.

I had never seen so many sparks and explosions. I covered my ears and muttered to myself for the pitiful drivers to shut up. Once the commotion had ceased, I walked between the accidents asking what had happened. When I reached the Citation, I knocked on the old woman's window.

Mam. Roll down. Please.

But the frail woman had not been wearing her seat belt. Her poor head had cracked through the windshield where it remained on the outside, neck twisted, face bruised, nose and eyes bleeding. She was quite flaccid.

My attention was again diverted by the windmills as I compared them to ballet dancers in unison. My torn door lay under the woman's car. Several people had begun to screech at me, for they had seen where my car was parked—in the middle of the highway.

You! screamed a large man in a tight t-shirt with a stomach like a bean bag. He pointed at me and charged up the dotted lines that divided the road.

There he is! a few others yelled.

I ran back to my stolen car as they kicked and punched me, their spit hitting me like shells emptying from a gun on a concrete floor. The big lesson here is not to stare at windmills on the highway, and if you do, make sure that you park on the *side* of the road. The doorless ride home was not very fun either.

An hour or so later, I arrived back in the city proper of Los Angeles. After exiting from the Hollywood freeway onto Alvarado, I passed several mexican and chinese owned garages, car washes and restaurants, and turned left on Marathon. I spoke no spanish but promised myself that I would learn soon. When the street elled with Coronado, I parked the car on an incline facing downhill.

A red and white sign above me said NO PARKING THURSDAYS 12:00 TO 2:00 STREET CLEANING. What day was it?

I reached over to open the door but realized there wasn't one. So I unbuckled my seat belt and stepped onto the street. Two mexican girls with long silk black hair in baggy pants and flannel shirts were carrying back packs. They pointed and laughed at me.

Nice dress, gringo!

They shouldn't have insulted my sartorial choices, but they did. I laughed back and pointed at them and crouched over to indicate my side was in physical pain from how much they made me laugh, even though I was just getting them back. They gawked at me like two kittens confused after licking a ball of red LSD yarn.

As I crossed the residential street, I wondered how I had gotten so far from home, all the way out to Arizona and back. Then I remembered: the place in the desert with the Joshua Trees. I had to go again.

It was a prophetic mission, a messianic job. Over the years I had seen that *mene* graffito on the wall just like in Daniel 5:25, the disembodied hand writing to me. At first, I was churlish as uncultivated desert sand about the matter, not listening to my visions, but their repetition had me reconsidering my seer status. See, I have this theory. I have been chosen, yes, but for nothing. However, nothing is god. By the transitive property of something or another, that means I have been chosen for god. I am nothing though. Somehow, I am driven by this cause. It's not nihilism. We are talking about a mindset here. Whatever. I don't even understand it myself. Moving on to the next subject.

How did I get lost in Arizona in the first place, is the question. Let's see, I thought, I got on the 101 South this morning and took it to the 110 South and then to the 10 West. Somehow, I found myself on the 605 South but made it back to the 5 going north, which ran me back into the 10 heading west, but accidentally I was sidetracked onto the 110 South, found myself going west on the 105, came to the 405 and rode it north for a few miles and returned to the 10, this time going east.

That's it, I said to myself: I stayed on the 10 East and was afraid I'd get lost again, so I just remained on it. Those windmills had caught my eye and distracted me.

I will leave this car right here and catch the bus. I think Sunset is over there.

Some other time I will go to the place in the desert. Often at the beach, sand calls me. Desert sand is different, lonelier than beach sand.

YOU ARE FLYING

Due to all the confusion I decided to clear my head with an airplane ride, now that I had so much money. Forgetting which city I requested to go, I bought a ticket. Everyone was quiet until the businessman next to me, you, receding pate, began to rip pages of paper in half. You fished through your briefcase, stared at a sheet and tore it slowly down the middle, causing everyone within five or six seats to ogle you in disbelief. You had drunk two glasses of whiskey and no telling how many more in the airport. My eyes were dry and I was tense.

The aisle separated you and me. I could imagine you at your desk in whatever fungible business you performed, repressing anything decent about yourself until you ended up raping your wife one night while she slept, like in *Rosemary's Baby* where the husband forms this pact with Satan to further his acting career and lets the devil impregnate Mia Farrow after she's been poisoned with drug-laced chocolate mousse.

Riiiiiip. Another page. You examine a sheet of paper, tear it in half. If you do it four more times, I will say something. I hold in what I feel for too long. Maybe you will misunderstand my tone when I finally express myself. Maybe you will not know how upset I am about losing my story in the magazine. You know nothing of my situation, only my disposition.

I can't stand you anymore.

Stoptheripping, I begged rapidly, stopityousonofasheepcopulation!

Ehh? you grunted.

Are you going to perform that maniacal tearing the whole trip?

Maybe, you snorted.

Your behavior is truly uncaring.

Z'it bugging you?

Yes, I responded. Z'it is.

Eventually you put your stuff away, ripping no more. I felt guilty. We had tension between us. You probably beat on your kids then forget about it the next morning. I know you are full of rage, just from your amateur ripping method.

Because I am too. I should feel compassion and forgive you, but I just don't like you.

Thanks, I said, being the decent man, for stopping.

Hey, dose were investment documents. Dey either had ta be shredded or torn up. I'm all done. I quit for myself, not you.

Ahh, I thought to myself, you didn't stop for me. I need to forgive you. I don't want to be on a plane crash. Where's the stewardess with my peanuts and apple juice? Once I have a snack, I will feel better. Hate is a chemical reaction to hunger. Do peanuts scare you? Their ubiquity frightens me. Where can you go and *not* find a peanut? Exactly. Nowhere. Peanuts, like nothing, might also be god since they are so scarily omnipresent. Oh, I once went into a men's room in Maryland and saw a transvestite. I am a terrible stalker. I can't remember what I'm thinking about. I need to work on segues and avoiding non-sequiturs. This plane will land soon and I will find another one of you. For now, I will write in my stalking journal.

I ended up in a city. I did not know where. I truly wanted to stay and begin a different life and forget who I had been previously. While I walked through the empty airport past all the slot machines, I realized I would never escape myself, that I was strange and unsociable and destined to be on the periphery. Everyone around me seemed to move through his or her life in an unconscious stupor, and only I noticed. If I explained the contrast to a random person who looked intelligent enough to discuss the matter, I was nearly always greeted with befuddlement, fear or the beckoning of a security guard.

Most people I approach look down on me. They welcome me for a moment in order to show how they stand above me, so they can tell their friends how they met someone *like* me, and then they use me as an example of a person who has lost sight of himself, and, whew, aren't they glad such insanity hasn't happened to any of them.

All I want you to see is my point. If I observe something, I want to share this information with you, yet you smirk at me. You nudge the guy next to you and say, *Look*. You are amused by my antics until they become a threat, until the honesty overwhelms and scares you. Then I'm not so funny, am I? I am the truth that you cannot endure.

I needed to go home. I needed to lose my money and be alone and poor again. I am mortally afraid of being mugged. Every night I dream of two men whacking me in the mouth as I round a corner and tearing my teeth from my head and asking me for all my cash.

Wait, what city is this? It didn't matter. I stayed in the airport and watched so many of you. Too much. You all were too much. Pathetic, but I never even made it out of the airport and found a flight back home as soon as I could. I was happy to spend more money to rid myself of it.

Back home again. We only have a couple of days before I go to find you. Of late, uncanny events have accumulated; I have been occupied in hopes of ascertaining their meaning. I have always been prone to coincidence, being oversensitive and believing fully in the intuitive magic that occurs when random events conjoin with no seeming purpose and yet overlap in so many layers of meaning as to defy logic. Though not attempting to rationalize the inexplicable, I am convinced these interstices must be deified eyes, something ineffable, to be sure.

For example, let's say you run into someone you know from your past. But what is the phenomenon that occurs when you happen to run into someone you never liked, and yet the feeling of recognition and nostalgia supersedes any animosity when you greet the person as if he were the finest acquaintance you have ever known? You are just happy to know that you have had a past, that someone from it (affable or not) has appeared to confirm your earlier history.

I buy used books a few times a month. Not an avid collector, I like to read authors who fall through the cracks—or are falling— and either give the books to someone else, sell them back or leave them to be forgotten on my own shelf. With some frequency I pop into used shops and buy what I like. I prefer to stroll at these times. I make more discoveries this way.

Walking up Fairfax the other day I found a new thrift store and entered. I searched for literary fiction and anything not by a celebrity. I picked out eleven books, some of which I had read, some I wanted to read. A treasure, I thought: eleven books for three dollars. I went to an Italian movie about a rich deaf man who follows a homeless man. After the film ended, I considered the events in my mind: finding some random paperbacks at the thrift store and choosing to read them instead of others. As I looked closer at one of the novels, I noticed it was about a schizophrenic man who *thinks* he follows another man, who ends up being himself.

Then I was trying to write my own work without letting these books permeate me. Cursed with foreknowledge, I was doomed to write the truth but have it scoffed. No one wanted to hear what I had to say, even though I knew the answer, which was not complicated. The answer was clearly: stalking.

In my bed I felt a surge of energy in my head that would not let me sleep. If I knew the future, why did I still try to understand it? Besides, I was bent on petty revenge of someone I didn't even know, concerning a story I had lost, a story that would be forgotten in time.

You must be the answer, I decided. You are the final link to this series of coincidences. I just need to find you. Whether I search for you or not, I will still meet you.

What is today? How long do I have? I do know the future. And—yes—you must know also! When you tattled on me at the newsstand, you must have known I would follow you and that I would leave you alone but only in order to come after you again.

Now I see. I'm not coming after you at all. We are meeting.

You and I.

We are supposed to meet.

For whatever reason. But we are.

I am forgetting temporal strictures, meaning that whenever I feel ready to come to the newsstand, I will. No longer am I controlled by when I should leave. When my intuition's voice speaks silent assurance is when I will go. Question is: what am I going to do until we meet?

I wanted to pay my landlord all the back rent. Much to his own surprise, Chester accepted the money. I decided to slide my remaining bills under the mexican man's door and work for a living. I still had three-hundred dollars and slipped it under his door with a forged note from the girl who had asked him to turn down his music volume. The note said, Here's three-hundred dollars. Now, turn down your radio FOREVER.

I waited for you, becoming less vengeful by the moment. A voice implored me to focus on a job. I bought a newspaper and looked at some of the abject vocations listed in the classifieds:

—Envelope Stuffer
—Customer Service Collections Agent
—Recycling Center Plastic Bottle Washer/Rearranger
—Chihuahua Nurse (what?)
—Deliverer of Organic Butter to Anarchists (?!)
—Missing Teeth Study Subject
—Pet Bird Plasma Donation
—Shrimp Processing Factory Conveyor-Belt Crustacean Flipper
—Calculator Key Repairman
—Tuna Fish Can Tester

At this point the newspaper ink had smeared my fingers and, for that matter, my psyche. Time for a different vocational plan.

YOU PAY FOR ME

I found a street corner, wore a pair of faded blue jeans and a tight t-shirt that said MOIST. At first, men, fat and in their fifties, stopped. Even though I really needed the money, I had some pride to maintain and told them to shoo.

My first customer was luxury vehicle, not a limousine, just a big American car. I remember how you rolled down your window to expose a haggard but chiseled face. This city is filthy, I thought to myself right before you pulled up. Litter on the streets, window panes coated with soot, bums on bus stop benches, strutting transvestites amusing the drivers stuck in traffic. I wondered why I chose to live here and not near a lake. In the city no insects land on your neck and bite you because the air kills them the second they enter the carbon-poisoned megalopolis. In this city you see no stars, even on clear nights. Cities are starless in the end.

I was too bizarre to be part of any real social world and thus was doomed to my condemned perception, my lucid awareness of everything disgusting and the inability to reject my fascination for it. I belonged nowhere, and since here was nowhere, I belonged here: on this sidewalk corner in my tight jeans, waiting for a woman like you who would pay for me. I didn't care about the money. I just wanted to hug someone. To be in a bed with a lithe body and experience all the smells of nervousness and lust. To touch slender legs. To place my ear against a stomach and stare at toes while a radio played good jazz softly (not soft jazz badly).

Why can I imagine what I want all too well, but when it comes to enacting the vision, I become lost, *so* lost I have no idea what I searched for in the first place? Have I failed in finding what compels me to imagine perfection? Or am I simply admitting how impossible it is to transpose a thought to reality?

As you drove, the car slowed but did not stop. Your passenger window droned down and your face leaned over to eye me. You were semi-famous for multiple commercials about cheeseburgers. Your peroxide teeth glistened. You had no real eyebrows but tattoos of them etched over your eyes. I found myself matching your pace and trotting as you inched the car along. Raising your tattooed eyebrows, you motioned me to join you. I nodded and was happy that I wouldn't have to deliver organic butter to anarchists. You stopped. Traffic flung past us like fists in a boxing match.

Inside the car you waited for me to give my terms. Having done no research, I had arrived at two-hundred dollars as a plausible sum. But since you appeared to be a woman of largess, I had no qualms about asking for five-hundred. Then I realized I couldn't do it at all and wanted to open the door and fall to the street and roll around until another car squished me, a child stepping on a jelly doughnut.

Three-hundred, I said, staring ahead.

You nodded and said nothing and drove west on Santa Monica, out of dingy Hollywood into neon boy's town of West Hollywood and past the gargantuan bronze statues and city hall mosque in Beverly Hills until the street ended, after thirty minutes, in Santa Monica. We turned left on Ocean and headed south to Venice but turned right after the pier and parked near the hanging rings that looked like empty faces.

I followed you, thinking you wanted me on the beach. Instead, you stopped at the rings, eight of them set up in succession. You stood on a platform, leaned forward to grip the first one and held it against your chest. You wore shorts and sandals. Your body under the night lamp yellow hue appeared tan and strong. Before I could finish admiring your legs, you had removed your shorts. They fell with a susurrus as you kicked them onto the beach. I pulled off my shoes and massaged the balls of my feet in the chilly sand grains. The waves seemed to gasp, then whisper, gasp, whisper.

I gazed at you standing on the platform. You said nothing. Your clothes lay strewn. Each ring was attached to a chain. Each chain stretched fifteen feet straight up and connected to a metal bar. The apparatus looked like an upside down V with the eight chains hanging down in a line. You hopped off the platform, slightly to the side and swung to your left, hanging onto the ring with your right hand. Your arm stretched straight. Your naked body was gliding as your left hand grabbed the second ring and you released your right hand to clutch the next one, and so your hands moved.

The chains swung behind you as you glided ahead. Were you strong enough to go to the end? And come back? It was difficult to return to the platform because the rings no longer hung still. They swayed from side to side and eluded you. I saw your shadow—for a moment you vanished—then you began to come back. I waited for you and wanted to know your name. You were not just a you.

Was this all you wanted?

Here you were on the platform again. The waves exhaled.

An angel, your small toes together. For free I wanted to say. I want you for nothing and yet would never know your name.

You unbuttoned my jeans and unzipped me and asked me to do the rings. I slid the pants down my legs, bark coming off a dead tree, and climbed the two steps to the metal platform.

Halfway through, I looked to my right and there you were, beside me, urging me on, jumping with excitement.

For each ring I grab—each time I progress—you will want me more. Won't you? The less I achieve, the worse I am. At the end, when it is time to turn around, I have to swing into the void. Facing the ocean for a second I know all the rings behind me are like chiming bells, back and forth, back and forth like the waves in front of me, and when I sail out, hanging onto the eighth ring, I know I will have to turn around very soon. You are there. My rotator cuff creaks in its socket.

Now the ocean is to my back and I face the chiming rings. I miss! I miss the seventh ring, which means I have to hold on and fade back toward the sea and try again and hope the seventh ring will be in the right place. This time I look up and see the stars, salty, very bright, and the seventh comes into my hand.

After that it is all fine. My back aches on five and four. My grip gives on two. On one, I want to quit, but I want you. With a lunge from my hips I heave myself onto the platform.

In the cool beach air I have shrunk and am embarrassed.

You take my hand.

We walk to the water, leaving our clothes behind. Some of the hanging rings still glide through the air on their own.

I want to maybe know you. Soon, all I will want is to be away from you, and when I am that, I will, again, want your nearness.

I place my foot near the water. You stay where it is dry and sit with your knees to your chin, your arms wrapped around your shins. My skin trembles when I think of the cold sand touching your body and a slight gasp renders me with no breath for a moment. You are a body and you wait for me. It will not be here on the beach that we touch.

You take me back to the rings.

We find our clothes and return to the car. We are naked on the seats. After you turn the ignition and the engine roars, we idle for a long time. The heat blows cold at first and you ask me to sing to you. You place my head in your lap. The car becomes warmer. My bones begin to lose their chill. Then we are feverish and I am trying to sing softly. You want something else.

Without any concern for my head, you bang the back of my neck on the steering wheel. You don't apologize. You cram my mouth between your legs and place both feet on the dash and instruct me to bite you. I begin to kiss the rim of your lips, already drenched from juices. You smack my cheek (hard enough to startle me) and peremptorily instruct me to bite, not kiss. You finger yourself and scratch my nose in the process. You smile and begin to drive. Stay down there, you moan, we'll be at my house soon. I wait for soon. My neck hurts and I don't move it. I let you control me, just like I used to hold gas in my stomach while in church.

Just at the moment I was about to lift my head, I felt your foot go for the brake and saw your hand reach for the gearshift.

We're home, you said, stay connected to me.

I continued to bite you as we clumsily extricated ourselves from the car. You made me crawl (partly dragged me) to the door, begging me to not stop. You yanked me into your kitchen and turned on the sink spigot and splashed your face. I continued to bite you softly. You flipped on the blender and opened the refrigerator and all the cabinets. This was all to keep you from falling. You smelled flowers on the counter. You bit the back of your own hand while I bit your thigh. You opened drawers and turned on the stove and pushed a button on the blender to make it go faster. You dropped knives and forks and spoons; they bounced and clinked in symphony on the tile. You poured a gallon of milk on the floor and drenched my hair. You poured orange juice on your breasts and shouted that we were under a citrus waterfall.

I finally pulled you to the cold floor but not before you had strewn cold grapes that squished on my back. Each sense was loucheful wrath. I could feel the sauna warmth of the stove. The silverware mixed with the milk and green grapes, and I was stabbed twice (once semi-anally) by fork prongs. While you sucked on me, you sat your vagina on my big toe and cooed like a hen pecking on a toothsome corn morsel.

The milk dried on me and began to stink. You located some bologna in the fridge and slapped slices of it on my back. In response, I unpeeled American cheese and clothed you with twenty pieces. We came and came. Amid our frolic, I made up a haikuish poem:

Where does it come from, the come?

Every day, I have some.

When I woke up and looked around and heard the noise of the blender and felt the heat of the stove, I could not move, nor could you.

You told me to look in your purse for my money.

Three hours later, after outrageous copulation, I did.

You had begged to drive me home.

I refused.

I would walk.

Stalking requires peregrination as ongoing practice.

I staggered homeward. Every muscle cried like a teething baby in a sour diaper filled with butternut squash feces. After my sadistic frisson with you, I wanted to walk in the night and be alone. I wondered about all the people in the world right then who were about to commit suicide. Sui. Of oneself. Cide from caedere, to kill. To kill oneself, hm, but the self doesn't die so easily, does it now? It remains in the memory of the living who knew you.

The body dies, certainly. The memory of you does not, as long as there are people who remember you. Therefore, only when those people die do you die, officially. Sorry suicide victims: you need to kill all your friends if you truly want to die.

One of the great things about life is your choices. You can die whenever you want, and nobody can do a thing about it. You can wake up one morning and tell yourself you are no longer worthy of this world and point a gun barrel at the roof of your mouth and wave goodbye to all of the people who judge and condemn you; who love you when you achieve nothing; who despise you when you have fame.

That is quite a power, to me, at least. Can a skunk off himself? No. He has to wait to be eaten by a predator. Skunks don't have guns like we do. They can't hang themselves either. We can. Do they have poison? No. A moose never thinks of suicide. Why? I'll tell you why. Because he eats grass about three hours every morning, then he sleeps for about six days. Why does he need to die when he's already dead?

Most everyone I know is a moose. They ignore their lives. They die in their food, or, worst of all, their futile jobs. Moose and skunks don't have to answer a phone and peck on a computer and make money to live, while barely able to pay for their food, rent and bills. They don't have to worry about having a car accident or being mugged (maimed by his predators maybe, never mugged). I want to be lizard. Or a cow. I haven't decided which. Even a cow has a purpose when she dies. We transform her hide into shoes. We also eat her. Do we get eaten? Except by worms in death, no. Why not? Why don't we eat each other? Do we taste bad? I think it's just awful to not donate our human meat selves to hungry animals after we spend all our lives eating them. All suicides should be fed to the animals.

When you think about it, human beings are hollow. We sit in the ground after we die and we sit behind a desk when we live. Everyone owns a desk. And what does a desk look like? Exactly. A coffin. Turn a desk upside down and take out the drawers and you could bury yourself in it. I'm all for suicide. And since I don't have any friends, I will die for real when I die. I don't mind my body being devoured by animals. I just don't mind, my friend.

Maybe I want to die. Are you going to condemn me for it? So you condemn my life, but when I tell you I am about to end the thing, your condemnation does not cease. Hah, I am a fool for listening to you then. If you consider each option wrong, life and death, you are probably behind a desk right now. Or have been within the last ten hours. You probably work as a tuna fish can tester.

People of the world: turn your desks upside down and die in them!

Hang yourselves from light fixtures!

Slice your wrists with kitchen knives!

Die because you died when you became boring.

Inhale something besides the ennui.

I have a long way to walk. Many of you will die and I will never know you. That means you will be forgotten as quickly as a crushed wasp under its vespiary. The highway is near me. I could step in front of a car. But I will walk. I will walk home. I need new shoes. I don't really want to commit suicide; it merely passes the time to consider it.

My penis hurts from our sex trapezing. Don't get me started on the penis. A car is a penis while also being a womb. That's why people get livid in traffic. They are inside a womb that is propelled forward like a penis. This womb-penis is very confusing. Think of all the womb-penises out there on the highways. Freud had this concept of penis envy which is basically when a young girl realizes she doesn't have a penis. A young boy has the equivalent castration complex when he figures out he has no vagina. The point here is that the womb-penis car reminds us of penis envies and castration complexes.

The hike was taking three hours, time enough for me to create another chapter devoted just to this walk. But the extra time was good in that the hypnotic strides relaxed my mind and allowed me to finally remember my story, the one in the magazine. Who was reading it, I tried to guess. Who had bought the last copy?

Okay, since you asked, I had written about this magic trick. About this little girl, Aurora, who can disappear when anyone is mean to her. Everyone wonders where she has gone and becomes worried until she reappears somewhere else. Anytime someone hurts her feelings, she vanishes. She has a deranged sister who follows her everywhere. The only trouble with Aurora's special legerdemain is the limited use of it: she can only disappear a finite number of times. Since the world is so full of execration for her, she has to flee often and use her skill often. Unfortunately, she has no idea when the last time will be.

Her mad sister yells at her and bites her without surcease. Right before their final confrontation, she purposely trips a man who begins to be mean to her, and, of course, when people are mean to her, she disappears. She notices her sister coming around another corner. As the little girl is fading away from the tripped man's anger, the sister finds her. The sister chokes her, but Aurora is half-vanished.

In the end the little girl only sustains a few bruises on her neck and she remains half-vanished for the remainder of her life as a reward for finally figuring out how to escape her sister's terrorism. However, she receives an even better gift: her sister believes her to be dead. Once she is no longer able to disappear, she finds that no one is mean to her anymore. In the unpublished sequel to the story, which, by the way, is called "Neither Here, Nor There", she learns how to deal with living as a half-vanished person.

I was almost home. Nearly mo(u)rning. The sun rose over the highway. I tried to stop thinking of penises and suicide. I did focus on the word "peer" and wondered how people who pee on you could be considered your friends. Awful word, "peer". Just awful.

Out of the blue I remembered this saint named Ephrem who was known as the "Harp of the Holy Ghost". Whenever he preached, his throat became so stopped with tears he had to pause. I don't know what made me think of him, except for the fact he was supposed to be very humble and is said to have never been angry in his life. How's that, I wondered. Never angry. I am half-cocked all the time; in fact, I am never not with rage.

The walk seemed to have no end.

Ah, a diner.

I stopped in and ordered the hottest coffee they had. A sad, wrinkled anile with varicose veins on her calves brought me coffee. I almost ended up in the hospital. I had a lapse of memory and was certain I was about to guzzle a glass of cold lemonade. Get this: I swallowed a whole cup of coffee. The liquid scalded my tongue and gums and caused aches in my teeth. I drank it to the bottom. If it weren't enough that I had lacerated the inside of my mouth as blood oozed onto my lip, my chest exploded with the heat and I screamed for someone to help me. I begged for ice water and guzzled it, not slaking my thirst.

All down my chest, heat pounded and coated my heart and ribs. The three waitresses scrambled around and tried to help me. I wanted to keep pouring hot cups of coffee into me. Was this a known means of torture? If not, why not? Drink a hot drink. Drink many.

Hours past before I calmed down. I rubbed ice across my chest. I swallowed whole cubes of ice and choked. Why had I thought it was cold lemonade? How could I make such an idiotic mistake?

You want to know the most insane thing of all: I wanted another cup of coffee.

How I woke up in an alley is beyond me. The stench of rubbish fetid as urine entered my nostrils and forced me to gag. I knew it was afternoon. They say that people who sleep through the morning are cut off from themselves because they are afraid to dream. I would have to agree. My tongue was burnt.

Emerging from the alley I was closer to my apartment than I had calculated. Checking my pockets to see if I'd been robbed, I promised to go to the health food store and drink one of those healthy shakes they blend together with all sorts of weird substances like bee pollen, bat scrotum, etc. I like to stare at the actresses and their long legs in tight pants and wonder about the short life of commercial beauty.

Since the health food store on Beverly was only a few blocks from my house, I think I must have glowed with pleasant happiness at the fact I wouldn't have to walk much further. The tall girls were everywhere, only, today, they walked right past me (filthy, I was). A few men smiled. I didn't want sex like their grins implied. I bought my shake, sucked my straw, calmed my tongue.

Suddenly, I overheard a commotion and turned around to see a homely woman yelling, It's not my juice!

Yes it is, the cashier replied, his coal black hair in corn rows.

It's the person's who just left. That's not my juice. Her proud profile reminded me of George Washington incused on the quarter.

I saw you, uh, drink—

Where is the manager?

A thin female strolled by me with resolve and tried to assess the situation. This is not my juice! echoed, causing a mild titillation among two hippies who were contemplating which brand of shark cartilage to purchase. An empty plastic cup, residue of liquid purple fructage coating the sides, sat on the black conveyor.

By now the whole store was silently watching as the woman pointed to the cashier and repeated that he was harassing her. I left quickly, sensing something wrong. Outside, the sun, strong and unforgiving, begged me to stare it in its eyes. Having no hat, I cupped my hand against my forehead. The effusive woman exploded through the doors behind me and rodeo-tackled me. She refused to apologize, and any sympathy I had managed to find for her in the store was lost. I watched her stomp on the sidewalk under her, a plastic bag carried in each hand.

Maybe she would go home and tell her husband how rudely she was treated and how she hated the city and everyone descending on her. Or maybe she would go home to no one and cry because she knew how absurd it was to argue over an empty cup of juice. I wanted to run after her and say I understood her frustration. She probably would think I was a pervert, though, and reject any solicitude I might offer.

I don't know about this morose little world sometimes. We are in proximity to each other, and yet we never connect. I see you heading toward me on the sidewalk and you don't move out of my way, and I think, *You wanted to lay your shoulder into me.* I feel you feeling it. We have rage in common and we prefer to replace it with silent bitterness.

On my way home I passed by several bizarre members of the public. A bum with bleached white hair and a very sunburned face stared at me.

Hi, I said.

Frogs are cute, he replied. And so are you.

I walked fast. Whenever I neared someone, I said hello. They said nothing. Did I not speak loud enough? After several attempts I quit.

One day you will all quit saying hello.

YOU WERE ALWAYS ON, MY MIND

In my apartment shower I let my head swim in the muffled noise of water pounding my skull lightly. I was ahead on my rent. What an effort it was to walk to the store and buy the food I needed, even though I was flush with money from selling myself. It's almost as if I didn't want to eat. The water coursed over my back and I turned around until the nozzle aimed at my stomach. With my loofah, I scraped away all the dead skin on my arms. Then my legs. Mmm the water.

The newsstand stayed open late. I had plenty of time. If you were there, watch out! Stop using exclamation points!!! JESus.

I dried my body and shaved and splashed cold water on my face to close my pores. Pouring rubbing alcohol into one cupped hand, I slapped my cheeks where I had shaven, under my chin and below my jaw. My skin tightened and the vapors billowed up my nose and I opened my eyes wide. In the mirror I saw a spider on the wall behind me. I lifted the plastic bottle of isopropyl and pointed the mouth at my target and doused the sorry arachnid (probably the same one that bit me the week prior). It slid to the floor and tried to stagger to safety, but I grabbed the vaseline, twisted off the top and scooped a handful of jelly gunk and stopped his octo-legs in his tracks.

I dressed. I found my knife and slipped the blade into my back pocket. I located bus fare. I waited at the bus stop. The bus came. I said hello to the driver and dropped my change into the slot. Erotic. The money fell with a jingle. I was the only one on the bus.

At the newsstand I saw you. You saw me. You didn't recognize me with my hair combed. Whatever surreptitious business you had with the proprietor last time, when you had me removed, was now immaterial. Showtime, my friend. Absolute showtime.

I looked just fine with my hair combed. You continued to read your porn mag. I moved closer to you. You waited. I was very close to you, about to ask you why you had interfered in my life, when you bolted abruptly into a sprint. I'll have to say with those stubby legs of yours you still run fast, although you're no Seabiscuit.

You approached the parking lot behind the newsstand and fumbled for your keys, and it reminded me of our earlier scene at the gas station. I followed you and stood behind your car. You said nothing. No apology. No remorse. As calm as I could, I came to you. You were so dumbfounded that you couldn't move. I won't hurt you, I thought, unless you hurt me. And then you did. You spat on me. I felt so degraded that I knew I had to strangle you— but not to death. Like the spider still squirming in the vaseline.

I wielded my knife and told you to open your trunk. You hopped in waving your hands like a woman in a horror movie. I slammed it. Still, you were silent. Maybe you spoke. I didn't hear you if you did. I turned your keys in the ignition. And I backed up slowly.

At the ocean near a deserted pier, I opened the trunk and placed the knife against your throat. The ferris wheel turned in the distance.

My story was in that magazine, I informed you.

You said you didn't know, you were sorry, you wouldn't do it again.

In my mind I gutted a slash in your stomach and a pig fell into your lap. Your guts were a pig. It made me crave ham with hot mustard. Mustard lowers your heart rate. While I daydreamed about ham, though, you snatched the knife from me.

Very clever, I noted. With nothing to lose, I strangled you and you gagged. You rose to your knees and stabbed me several times in the arm above the elbow, as if chipping ice. Instead of feeling those wounds, I began to understand how severely my tongue and throat had been burned by the coffee last night. I was thankful for the perspective on my pain. My grip relaxed. So did yours. It was good to know you only wanted to defend yourself.

Go, I instructed you.

The sky changed slightly and looked like a grandmother in a light blue Sunday dress bending over to smell a lavender iris.

No, you insisted, I want to take you to the hospital.

I refused and walked away from you. When you followed after me with the knife, I pointed to you and screamed, YOU STABBED ME! A girl shrieked. My bleeding arm, numb, was of no concern to me. You continued to follow me until a policeman saw us. He nabbed you.

Explain that knife now, buddy.

My plan was an obvious accomplishment. I had actually factored in the stabbing as a subterfugic stratagem.

We also learned this in stalking training.

I got off the bus at Union Station and went to the restroom where I splashed cold water on my gashes. I wanted to buy some rubbing alcohol. There were no stores to be found. I walked up and down the main streets and was about to pass out dizzied by the tall buildings. I sat down between two trash cans in an alley. Must have kipped off without knowing it.

When my eyes opened I couldn't remember where I was or why my arm hurt. Barely able to stand, I used the brick alley wall for support. Finally staggering up, I saw tiny points of light dotting the air in front of me like lightning bugs. I braced myself for a fall.

I noticed the blood on the side of my shirt and the pool around my feet. As I emerged from the alley staring up at a skyscraper, I saw that parts of downtown were immaculate, others like a landfill. People, mostly black and hispanic, stared at me or ignored me. None said hello. A few were shocked by the blood. No one, for the most part, noticed.

You got your revenge, my friend, but I'll bet you told that policeman who I was and how I attacked you. They'll be looking for me right now. Quite a surprise that they hadn't already located me.

At some moment I had ceased to worry about myself. This made death quite easy to stomach. When I turned the corner and saw them, I knew this was an altruistic opportunity. Four young men kicked an older man who was on the ground on all fours. They kicked and kicked, and every so often, since they all kicked at once, their feet would connect with the body at the same time and kick in unison for a few seconds, then the haphazard kicking took over once again. They kicked his face, his stomach, his back. He was a thick man and said nothing, only grunting with the blows.

They wondered who I was, tilting heads to sides. I took in their faces and decided to maim every one of them if I ever saw them again. One of them walked to me and, raring back, punched my chest so hard I wheezed for a breath. He laughed. Which is when I ducked and sent my head into his stomach, knocking him backward and bringing the other three down as well. Two of them elbowed me. I was past hurt, beyond feeling, flailing. With the heel of my hand, I detoothed one of them, recalling a baby tooth of mine dangling in its socket by a string of gums.

All of a sudden a weight crashed on all of us. It was the man they had been kicking. He and I battled them in puddles of blood. One got away, leaving three for us. I raised my wounded arm and poked as many eyes as possible. When it was over, everyone left. I crumbled to the ground, expecting to die. This was my time. I wanted it, it wanted me and I knew I was ready.

Of course, nothing happened. Only when I didn't care for death would it come to me, reminding me of its presence. I wanted death too much. When I wanted death not at all, then, then, it would mean I wanted life. If I wanted life, death would gladly take it from me. Since I didn't want my life, death laughed at me and told me to wait.

I have no blood left, but I will live. I stumbled around, vision blurring. My legs ached so badly I wanted to fall to the ground every few steps. I wanted to go home. Why had I given all of my money to the mexican man? I needed a friend.

I guess night was here and nobody was on the streets. Nobody ever is after walking in L.A. after nine o'clock, except me of course. My apartment! I needed to be there and pour some peroxide on my wounds. Besides, the gashes were small.

My horrible shoes increased my leg and lower back pain. Just when I wanted to give in, just at the moment I thought I wanted to stop and die, a tall man, a giant, came at me. I only saw his ursine size. His hair, greasy and uncombed, fit his harried appearance. Perhaps he worked as a mechanic as I gathered from the grease on his hands. A bike leaned against his body, an orange beach cruiser with a basket.

You wanna buy a bike? he said.

I don't have any money, I told him.

How much you got?

Certainly not enough for a nice bike like this one.

How much you got?

I told you: none.

Check again, Pedro.

Okay. My name's not Pedro.

I searched my pockets, more out of fear that he would kill me if I didn't. I came up with three dollar bills.

Three dollars, I announced, holding them up.

Any change?

I fished around for a few cents—sixty-three to be exact.

After counting, I told him I had a total of three dollars and sixty-three cents.

You got a deal.

Wha—

This back tire needs air, he informed me.

But, hey, is this on the level?

What do you mean?

Where did you get this bike? I asked.

Aww, I put 'em together at the bike shop where I work.

Really?

Straight up, he said.

Why are you selling it for under four dollars?

I need to get something to eat.

Well . . . all right, I said, and handed him the money.

The bike, except for the back tire being flat, was very nice and clean. I really liked the basket on the front.

He took the money voraciously. Thanks, now I can get that food I said I needed. I'm hungry.

I don't have any more money, I said, looking at him.

Say, you're arm is bleeding.

Thanks for the news flash at six.

Now I can eat a burger or something, he repeated.

You do that, I informed him, and rode off, back tire flapping in the wind. Actually, there was no wind. It hit me that I had around three-hundred bucks in the bottom of my shoe from my night with you and the exploding forks all over the kitchen. I turned around and found the giant and gave him this money. Who cares. I liked the bike and despised money. I parked it in a special hidden area.

I LOVE YOU?

At home I swabbed and cleaned my wounds and watched the spider's legs wiggle in the vaseline. Man, you're still living? Nice. Contrary to what I fancied, I lost very little blood. War wounds always inspire bigger stories than the scars themselves.

For three days I fell into a long sleep. Every time I tried to wake up, the comfort of the mattress and soft sheets wooed me back to bed. I didn't have much hunger, except for the occasional canned lima bean craving which I cooked on the hot plate, only to thereafter want nothing to do with them. Lima beans bear a close resemblance to congealed allergy mucus.

I was back to myself again with nothing to do, no one to bother, no real life, except for the general waking and sleeping and eating. No exercise. I read and waited. I waited for miracles to occur.

With you and all that newsstand trauma out of my life, I was without a purpose. I fixed the tire on my bike and rolled around the city. I waved to people but received no greetings in return.

I decided to bother the housewives in Beverly Hills. At first I posed as the phone repairman. Since most of these women have married for money and are cursed to live desolate lives of shopping and raising their children (while full of resentment for husbands who dangle money in front of their faces), they are eager to have scores of extramarital affairs to combat hubby's nailing of babysitters under the pool gazebo.

After seducing you in your bedroom, I heard children outside and asked if you were married. You said your husband was dead as far as you were concerned but had left you with two girls and a boy. Outside, I heard their din of laughter, the commotion of their infancy, and I wanted to marry you as you rubbed your fingernails across my stomach.

I had met you at dusk while I walked near a small lake few know is there. I saw you by yourself, arms crossed. I waited for you to walk around the pond. When you saw me, we spoke about nothing and both felt we could know each other.

You took me to your mansion, hidden by trees but close to the street. We walked around your yard. What we discussed, I don't remember, but we knew what was in store.

That next morning I discovered your children and loved them immediately. I shared my jokes and put them on my shoulders and made funny faces just to see them smile. I breathed in their germs and mussed their hair. The girls were pretty and eager to please, the boy quiet and sullen. They took care of one another and said the boy missed his father very much, which made me sadder than I know how to express. I wanted to be his father or to find his real one.

For many weeks I lived with you and your children. Weren't we something? I took them to school in your car. You trusted me with your house. You bought me a typewriter and a pen and reams of expensive manuscript paper. You made me write you something every day and tell you every image in my dreams relating to your body. Sometimes, while I sat at my escritoire, you massaged my shoulders. I all but forgot about my old place.

One day you helped me move out of that woebegone apartment. I said goodbye to none of my neighbors because I knew no one but you. I had no connection save to you. Even when I required solitude I wished for you by my side. Your smell transfixed me. Besotted as you made me, you managed to be drunker than I. Your children said you were different. How you added spices to their food. The food was fresher! You cooked more. You touched each child more, but most of all you touched me, and each time one of your fingers brushed my skin like silk, I shivered with so much pleasure that I only wanted to age with you and kiss every wrinkle on your body until we expired in one breath.

Our children (for you allowed me to make them mine) loved you and me. It was no surprise to either of us when you asked me to marry you, and since we both said it at the exact moment, neither of us heard what the other said, but we were synchronous and our rhythm was pure and exact. We agreed only to be married in spirit, exonerating us from the fetters of pseudo-ceremony.

Then, well, you saw me for who I am. Since my body is not used to love, it rejected what you gave me with spite. As if poisoned by what you offered, I exorcised your pulchritude through words. I needed hatred from you. Every day I feigned love for you and your children in order not to disappoint you. At night, my acting reviled me, though, and sentences would pour from me like a dump truck emptying sand.

When you began to read my writing, you saw some things about yourself you disliked. I tried to explain to you that I wrote them because to say them to your face and hurt you was impossible, for I did not want to spoil our life. The perfection we had was tenuous, as we both knew, and required much discipline. But I never wrote words to hurt you; in fact, I wrote them to not hurt you.

You still remained constant. You never altered.

I did. I soon turned against you, and you wondered why. You begged me to seek help. I did. You implored me to take drugs to calm me down. I did. You said I might write better. I wrote nothing at all. I cared not to write on the drugs.

Yes, we were very happy again. Or so you thought.

I shut off. My absence riled you to awful extremes. If my recounting of it is blank, that is in fact what my reaction was: not indifferent, not shocked, just blank. You dug your fingernails into my arm so that I still have scars. You bit my fingers while I slept. I awoke to your laughter, your teeth sunk into my hand. You tossed a glass of wine on my clothes saturating my white cotton shirt like a communion wafer. You ripped up my favorite book.

Having nowhere to go, I set up my typewriter at the pond where we met. I placed it on a large flat stone. For many weeks you brought me food. You left it in a place for me. One day a plate filled with spaghetti. Sometimes two halves of a cantaloupe. Insects bit tiny white moguls on my neck. You were no longer there to massage my shoulders. Each day the pile of paper grew, pages blowing onto the pond and landing on the water where they floated like face-down dead bodies.

You were supposed to leave me food, but you sneaked around the pond and begged me to stop the writing. The children missed me.

But I have met someone new, you informed me.

Fine, I said, fine, and continued to type about you.

Coming up beside me, you ripped the paper from the carriage and read my words, not believing for an instant that it was all about me, nothing to do with you.

There I am in words, you shouted like a rock through a window. You slapped the paper. You crumpled it into a ball and threw it into the pond where it floated away, Moses in his cradle. You pounded my back with your fists. You ran from me and left no food the next day.

I didn't get food from anyone else. In the nights I cried, wished for you. I was not myself. You needed someone less chimerical. I wanted to be alone and yet I wrote only about you, in order to one day return to you.

You convinced me to leave the pond and come into town to a café for a talk at night. I told you I was not very good at night. I warned you not to bring me there tired. I was tired. Covering my legs were white mosquito bumps from the pond. We sat in old arm chairs near a faded red pool table, sipping espresso.

I told you that I could not forgive you because I did not know how. Then I stood and ran because I knew I was becoming violent in myself. After I sprinted up my former street, near my old apartment, there you were. You had followed me. Why did you laugh at me? You wanted me to hit you, but I would not. You were always trying to get me to hit you.

We stood staring at each other on the sidewalk, not speaking.

I am not a very good man. What I see is not what everyone else sees. I notice only the sick; it is here that I feel content and safe. Those who are not sick mean nothing. They (you) are the mediocrity. They know nothing of me. They, however, are readers of my words. The sick do not read me (the sick don't need to). The mediocre sadly decide if my writing is correct, accurate, true. They decide, not the sick. The sick do not decide. The mediocre do. The sick and mediocre, sharing the roles of parasite and prey, are only separated by words, and, inevitably, my words.

I need a great war to know myself. I have never defended anything. I never fought for anything; hence, I was never hurt for a cause, and because I was never hurt, I am forever wishing for the war that would have saved me. You were shocked and puzzled that I needed writing more than you yet also needed writing to come back to you.

It's just a hobby, you retorted. Your writing is a hobby. Why try to make it something it's not?

A hobby!

Why don't you ever try to be beautiful? you asked.

I don't love this, I sighed.

I don't either, you admitted.

You left me alone for many days. Faithfully, you brought me food.

Part of me wanted to see you. I wanted to come back inside.

I avoided you for many days.

I left the pond altogether.

I had returned to my old apartment, which, not surprisingly, was still waiting for me. I sat at my desk in the small room and ignored your knocks on my door. I typed on a typewriter. About you. Sheets of manuscript paper were taped all over the room. The walls were covered with words. The knock was faint, accompanied by your soft voice. Then you began to beg on the other side of the door. This lasted for some time. Finally, my typing stopped. Frustrated, I began again, only to hear another knock.

There's no one here, I hissed, suppressing a shout.

Let me in. Please.

Go away.

Please.

No.

I have come to see you, Kit. I worry about you. Are you eating?

Leave me *alone*.

Okay, okay, goodbye.

While I left for a short walk, you broke into my small apartment and read what I wrote of you. I returned in time and caught you. I tried to explain my thoughts to you. Line by line I showed you my emotions. Still, you argued with me about my own feelings. You used my written words and my feelings against me when they were meant to stay private. Finally, I asked you to leave me in peace.

But you still lurked behind my door in the hallway. I heard you listening to me write. For a while. At some point I felt you leave me. There was silence at the door. Nobody there. You were gone. For many days I never knew when I fell asleep or awoke. I became exhausted from writing too long. My bowels, irregular and painful and anxious, controlled me. I sat on the commode and groaned and strained and cried from agony. I don't remember what I wrote. I couldn't figure out how to straighten my path, overgrown with weeds, gullied from rain, treacherous for footing.

For a week straight I woke at the same time, ate at the same time, fell asleep at the same time, napped at the same time, had an afternoon snack at the same time. My life changed for the better. I shaved at the same moment every morning. Had my tea at the same hour, right after my shower. I checked my mail, little that I received, every day at four. I stopped wearing dresses. I put my knife in a drawer. Even my eyes seemed less crossed.

Soon, I was rigid. If I missed a meal at lunch, or, for that matter, just missed having the meal at the appointed hour, I worried that the ripple effect would mar my sleep that evening. When it did not, I praised the glory of a schedule. Nothing altered me. I even found a job emptying gorilla piss at the zoo.

All of my days were exactly the same. I had come to the right! I even ate the same food every day. I washed and dried my laundry every Sunday at six p.m. If I listened to music or read a book, I did it in the mornings from ten to twelve. I read the paper at eight a.m. and did the crossword at nine.

Recognize me now? I doubt you do. I was on schedule. No unseen interruptions of emotion or feeling. I went through my days in regularity. My bowels improved. My writing turned optimistic. People on the street noticed my ebullience. They wanted to talk to me. I talked to them too. They had schedules just like me! They had jobs. They shaved their beards and legs at the same time in the morning. Meals occurred at the same time. Sleep, as well.

I identified with the world in a way I never had. I now knew how to be mediocre. Since there was no time allotted for anything but my life, I saw or required no need for extraneous activity, although I did exercise. I rode a stationary bike for thirty minutes, a wonderful metaphor for going nowhere. My agenda, the list of things I needed to do each day, in fact, never changed. A week passed. Then two.

During the time allotted to personal reflection, ten minutes after my morning hot beverage, right before I rushed to work, I napped for a few minutes. You might ask how I could nap during personal reflection, but when you're on a schedule, you multi-task!

I have not changed any. I am exactly the same every day, what I have always wanted to be. I have forgotten you from the newsstand. And you in your mansion who loved me but read my private journals. I have forgotten you who swung from the rings and poured milk on the floor and squished grapes under us and paid me money for my body.

I am different from then. Today I am unchanging. I take no vacations. I have no time for death. I write the same amount of words each day. I receive the same amount of mail every afternoon because I send myself a letter every morning. In these letters, I write about my past so that I may one day be able to dismiss it. You have no place in my life now. There is no time to remember you. Any of you.

One day I started stalking myself, though. I don't quite know how it happened. I think it was the rigid schedule that was causing me stress. It started with a look in the mirror. After that, I was irritated with myself and began following me. I followed me everywhere. In the grocery store I would look behind me, only to turn all the way around realizing I that was already in pursuit of me. Turning circles in the frozen fishstick aisle looked eccentric to say the least.

Stop following me! I said to me.

No, I said back to myself.

I'm not having this conversation, I informed me.

Um, yes, you are.

Okay, I'm having this conversation, but I don't want to be having it.

I would not quit. I followed myself for many days. Nights were the worst. Down a dark, dangerous street, I was always looking behind me. Sure enough, there I was. I didn't like being stalked, but it did give me some empathy for how all of you might feel when I follow you.

One afternoon, I was at a café and gulping down shots of espresso. I think I had ordered and slurped down about fourteen when my adrenaline from the caffeine had me quivering like a dog excreting a peach pit. Keep in mind that I was still on my schedule and acting "normal". In fact, I was writing in public and looking around to make sure everyone could *see* I was writing; this is what a lot of amateur writers do in cafés. I often notice them in coffee shops looking around and *not* writing. But, hey, I was embracing mediocrity and this was a part of it. Of course, I had gone overboard with the fourteen espressos and was just caffeine paranoid now.

I had to stop tracking myself. The upside to following me was that I maintained focus and had no stalking commute. Was this the Zen mastery of the stalker: self-stalking? I was coming apart at the same time, however, and blamed the schedule entirely. I tried to write in the café, but the proletarian talent here was bothering me.

Outside, the sun smacked my eyes. I spent the rest of the afternoon stalking myself, which is exhausting. You have to be the stalkee and the stalker, and that takes a lot of energy. I followed myself into random places. There was no chase but an internal one. I followed me into the mall. Do not *ever* go into the mall when you are self-stalking. Let's just say that I had a bad experience at a sushi restaurant, and we'll leave it at that. Basically, I don't want to talk about it, but when I sat down to order, my stalking self wanted miso soup and my stalkee self craved hot and sour. I started an argument then a fist fight, all with myself, and a female security guard rushed me out of the building, as I vehemently argued with me.

In the coming days, I was despondent. Like an elevator without cables, I fell. And the speed with which I descended roared with velocity. Screws popped out of their place. Metal sheered. Sparks popped with dots of light. I returned to sleeping until exhaustion and to never being coherent while awake. I wrote two words one morning and thousands in the afternoon. I punched myself in the face a lot.

The schedule! What a farce. I put so much into the strategy of ordering my life. And for what? My stalking had become onanistic and psychically masturbatory. I was a human-sized genitalia stroking myself into false orgasms, for I had lost the stalking path. In the end, stalking was about ethics, but the self(ish) had replaced my bailiwick of helping others. I was screwed in the worst ontological way. And the physical fights with myself were not as bad as the philosophical discussions. I just couldn't stand listening to me anymore.

I had to move and refocus. And I did. I moved.

I will confess I had sort of stalked this couple prior to moving in next to them. They took my mind off me, but I'm afraid they became a different extreme. Let me explain. First, "they" were in the third-person plural, not the second-person plural "you". I couldn't not even focus on the you! I was relegated to the "they". I would get back to you eventually.

Listening with an ear against my bedroom wall, I overheard an argument in their apartment next door. The walls were thin plywood.

It sounded like Guy's voice: I'm going to strangle myself and you'll have it hanging over your head for your whole life.

Kill away, she challenged. The she was Kitty.

They argued a lot in their bedroom.

You never listen to me, Guy whined.

And I'm thinking to myself: that's all they ever do, listen to each other. They never go out. They just sit around and listen to each other. They never work. I know because I never go out either.

I have a loud laugh and it just blurts outs. When this happens, I cough in the hopes they will think the laugh was a cough. Then they get quiet. They try to whisper for a while. Pretty soon they are at the yelling again and forget about me.

Most of the time they argued about this girl that Guy had once liked. From what I gathered, he had the hots for someone who was limited in the brain department. Even though Kitty was a knockout, I heard her talk about how many wrinkles she had or how her boobs were saggy. She lived to be good to him, to make herself a perfection. By the way I never heard them have sex.

Stop worrying about what you look like and realize that I love you for who you are.

Oh God, she spluttered, you are so full of it.

It's true, he said.

It's the tritest thing I've ever heard, Kitty said.

Tritest?

It's a word.

I don't think so, he said.

Let's look it up. I know it's a word because I checked. Right next to "tritheism" in Webster.

Oh, like you can call the dictionary by its first name.

They yelled about forty thousand decibels above normal hearing range and these arguments went on without termination. At some point, Kitty ran outside with her keys and threatened to go for a drive. Guy chased after her because she typically got in an accident if she drove after an argument. It happened twice and, each time, she had a new car within two days.

Often he tackled her. After they sat on the ground for a long serious talk, they came back to the apartment. One time they caught me looking out my window. Guy saw me and shot me a middle finger so hard that he knuckled my window and spider-webbed the glass. They never offered to pay for the repair. Whatever.

Sometimes I called from my apartment when they argued just to interrupt them. On the phone I'd say something like, This is the pizza place and our delivery boy should be there in a few minutes with your six pineapple pizzas. Click.

Kitty and Guy would emerge to glance around the balcony—we live on the third floor—and see no one there. If I felt gutsy, I would also go out and say, Waiting for my damn pineapple pizza, looking around for the pretend pizza boy.

It wasn't very good stalking, I'll admit, but I had to mount that horse again after my disastrous self-stalking nadir. I knew how to help them: barge in every once and a while and deflect their attention from each other. After all, I lived next door. I've always wondered how people can live so close together and hear other people's problems and never help. They don't. We don't. You don't.

Summoning my courage, I walked to my door, opened it and stepped onto the balcony. I *almost* used their knocker. Hearing them near their door, I stopped myself. I went back to my own apartment, knowing that if I had just rapped once, I might have disrupted their fighting, a wrench stopping the cogs. It reminded me of us, you and me, the way you stood outside my door and argued with me on the inside. I wondered how the children were.

It happened Tuesday. Kitty and Guy had kept me up all Monday night. I didn't mind since I guess I'm some sort of an aural Tom, something like a peeping Tom that hears. It was pre-stalking at best. I was still in the stalking minors. At this point I wasn't angry at them anymore for preventing my sleep. I was scared. Guy had talked a lot about suicide. Oh stop strangling yourself with the ankle wrap, I would hear Kitty reply to him. Poor Guy just wanted some attention from her, I guess. She was upset about not being able to get pregnant. Guy assured her that she could, if she truly wanted a baby. Guy was bankrupt too while Kitty had won on a huge insurance settlement, making her the breadwinner, further damage to his male-provider ego. They would sit in their house and talk in a circle about their problems. It wasn't like they left during the day for their jobs; they were there *all the time*. They took my mind off me, to be honest.

Tuesday morning, three a.m. The bedlam had kept me up all Monday night. Guy sounded like he was hanging himself again.

Get that belt off your neck, Kitty demanded.

My bathroom was adjacent to theirs, remember. I often heard them peeing or running water. I have this recurring dream in which a fight takes place and a man cracks open his head on the bathroom tile. I hate bathrooms. They are by far the worst room in the house.

Get down, Guy.

I heard a jolt and imagined that the belt tightened, a constriction around his neck.

How's that feel?! Kitty screamed.

A smash followed and then a tinkle, probably a light bulb?

How does that *feel*? she kept at him. Her voice bounced through their bathroom into mine.

I don't want your money! Guy spluttered.

Liar, Kitty goaded him.

Maybe I'll cut off my testicles and give them to you. Save you the trouble of castrating me.

Hang away. Go ahead.

What if I did like that girl?

Oh, don't you bring her up.

That nubile young girl, he continued. I'm a man, you know.

This is not good, talking about my friend.

What if she and I did do what we did? I'm so sorry, Kitty. You can have one if you really want one.

I don't *want* any kids. Not yours especially.

I did it because I hated you at the time.

She was close friend to me, Guy.

I know.

I wanted to have what she had with you. I wanted what she had and threw away.

She didn't do it to spite you. She just didn't want the baby.

Kitty became quiet.

I'm going for a drive, she threatened.

No!

She left.

I ran from my bathroom and watched from my window. She huffed down the concrete walk, down the stairs and over the sidewalk to her car in the parking lot. In his boxer shorts with no shirt, Guy ran after her with a baseball bat. That belt was still around his neck. He ran toward her, and I braced myself. She jiggled the door. It didn't open. When she saw him with the bat, she ran. He demolished the car, all the windows, the hood. In the distance she paused to watch him for a moment then fled.

That's when I decided to follow them closer. I tailed them across the street to the park, making sure they didn't see me. I hid behind a maple trunk and watched. It was early in the morning. Around four a.m. by now. The lights in the park hummed in brightness. Autumn was turning into winter. A pine smell filled my nose. I was barefoot and walked across a blanket of cushioning needles to see them argue.

Through gentle talking, Kitty won the bat from Guy and promised to forgive him for getting her friend pregnant. As I watched Kitty raise the weapon over her head and lower in fast monotonous repetition, I stood immobile as Guy begged her to stop, his hands covering his face like a child being whipped by his father.

Kitty sat by herself afterward. The bat lay on the ground. I wondered what she planned do with his body. I thought she might realize what she had done and break down. Instead, she stood again, took the bat and continued to bash Guy on his torso, as if she had not been grieving her deed at all but merely resting. She pummeled him on the top of his feet, on his forehead, on his shoulders. I heard thumps and cracks and saw this catatonic stare on her face. The rapid bat fell like an ax chopping wood.

When done, she stopped and panted and spun herself in a few circles, holding the bat with both hands and heaving it like a hammer throw in the Olympics. I watched that bat lift itself and disappear. My eyes lost the image in the lights.

Kitty walked back to the apartment.

I followed.

Back at her place the door stood open. She told me to come in and close it. I pointed to my apartment to indicate that I was just on my way home.

Don't leave, Kit. Please.

I have no idea how it happened so fast, but before I knew it, she charged toward me. I moved aside deftly to see her pass through her door, jump the railing and fly through the quiet morning air like a diver, just like a diver with a vacant face that I understood. And I believe I heard her whisper, *Useless life*.

After she smacked the concrete below, I went into my apartment.

I waited for just a moment.

I shut the door.

When the police knocked hours later, I told them I had been sick to my stomach all night. If there was a ruckus, I was unaware of it.

Did I know that my neighbors had both died violently?

No, no, I did not, I assured them.

The last thing I said before I shut my door in their face was something to the effect of not being the type of person who made other people's business my problem. A horrible lie. Absolutely the most horrible lie I could have told.

It seemed impossible to lose weight, given the heaviness in me. I vomited for no reason and cried. I longed for my old schedule, for living right, for salubrity. The evenness of life.

Again I walked the side streets and sold myself without care. Have you ever vomited for no reason? You just puke and laugh because there is no explanation—and you cry because you are doing everything you can to understand what is in you.

But answers don't come.

Are you vomiting because you have brainwashed yourself to be the same as everyone?

Are you vomiting up your lie, the mendacity of believing what everyone else believes?

You know full well that to accept their norms is wrong.

Their norms are not you.

When the blood jettisons from your mouth, what is that? If the vomit is the lie, what is the blood? Is the blood your life announcing itself as acceptable, your wanderings as fine? Can you choke up confirming blood when the acid of vomit spews onto the ground, telling you to believe in your blood? Reject your vomit, yes, it must come, for it is not you. Vomit is what others put in you. Blood is your own. Your blood will never come. It is within you and will stay, pushing out the vomit.

There you are, me, in an alley so similar to other alleys, sitting in pools of myself to save myself. I cover my face in shame and awake to . . . you. A stranger, a caretaker. You say you want to look after me. You tell me to follow you home. And I do. I feel very old. Who are you? Just someone who cares?

In your bathroom mirror I gaze at my face. After you wash the soot and blood from me, I see who I am.

You live by yourself. You have no one. You need me. You ask me to stay with you. You are different than they are. I tell you of Guy and Kitty. You listen. I tell you other stories. You say that I will never see the world as others do but only as it is. You tell me that I will always be alone. Your voice addressing my fears is a salve, mollifying me, soothing my wounds of insecurity. Why do I have a lack of credence in what I believe to be right, which is still a constant source of doubt? Why is my writing a disease?

You took care of me. What was your name? I never asked you who you were when you found me in the alley. You fed me, but I appreciated you barely. I left all the time. I came home late. You were so patient. For what were you waiting? For me to change?

Thank you for your house and letting me stay until my bruises healed and my stomach strengthened.

You caressed my forehead at night and told me I would be better one day. You never laughed at my writing. You were okay with me. I lived with you for longer than I had planned.

You said that I roamed from my feelings. You touched my knee and placed a cool washcloth on my forehead and wanted to calm me. You said that I talked like a jackhammer. I looked at you. Tilting my head to the side, I noticed your kindness. I asked you if the anger sneaked up on you like it did on me. In one moment, I said, you pet the cat, ooo, gitchygoo, her is a cute dittle precious . . . but then a man walks too close to you on the sidewalk, leaning into your space and you want to pulverize him, but you just don't understand it, him or you. You invent that you are claustrophobic. You feel powerless and you insist on forging your false strength, and this merely causes your bitterness to be more inscrutable.

You are losing weight, you warned.

You told me to close my eyes. You crossed the living room into the bathroom and re-wet the cloth that had turned warm. You brought it back to me. Now it was cool again, and I sighed when the wetness touched my skin. Thank you.

You are delirious, you said.

And I laughed.

You are pale, you said, touching me, always touching me, laying your fingers on me like the unseen toes of a butterfly. Is "butterfly" a spoonerism for "flutter by"? "Flutter by" seems more appropriate.

And you are dying, Kit.

Water fell from your eyes and I hesitated. I touched the wetness and placed it on my tongue and tasted the saline and knew you were crying for me.

You are—

Do not die, you begged. If you do, I will have nothing to care for.

Help me eat, I asked.

I have been.

I can't.

I began to die. For many weeks. Each time I was certain my heart had stopped or my will had acquiesced, I awoke with extreme anxiety. Even though I knew I was safe in your quiet house, protected up in Beverly Hills, I sensed danger. I wanted to do odd things to myself, such as go on job interviews. I had many days of delirium, syrup in my eyes.

My skin shed off me like a snake, the weight dropping from me.

I wanted to see all of you before I went.

But I knew you were in jail. It didn't seem right that you were there just because of a stupid literary magazine. There was that arm-stabbing though.

And you, ah you, were with your two daughters and son. I had grown fond of you, of them. I had not missed anyone like you in a long time.

You, my generous healer, however, were right in front of me. I gave you nothing and I took you for granted. You knew I wanted nothing from you, only to have you put that washcloth on my forehead. You read French to me even though it sounded very much like Spanish. I appreciated your kindness. It is what I wanted all my life, just didn't know how to accept it.

As a child I had an aunt who told me that as a man I would need but two things. First, a sword. Second, a harp.

The sword to make me heroic and courageous.

And the harp? I asked my aunt.

The harp, for your fingertips.

My fingertips?

Touch the strings, she added. Make quiet music.

I feel as if I have lost them both, having held onto the sword longer. Last year I wanted to call my aunt and ask her where I could find them. How could I get them back? I had a certain prowess with the sword and an admirable gentleness with the harp. I wrote you a letter, aunt, and I waited for you to send me word, to let me in on the secret of recovering what is lost. But I never heard from you. I even rode a bus to where you were, but you were not there. I made some calls to your sons and daughters; they were nowhere to be found.

I still don't know where they are, harp or sword. I make no music and I have no courage. I will find those tools. I must. I believed in my sword and just when I had used it a little too much, just when it no longer served me, I found my harp for balance. Yes, there were times I played too much music, and of course there were many times when I sliced through too many things, yet all in all I used them properly and equally, and I can't comprehend where they went, if they disappeared because I no longer needed them, or they were taken away from me since I ceased to use them as they should be used.

I need them again.

Aunt . . . ?

You saved me by listening to me, touching me. I lived, weakly, and did not die. I still don't see so well sometimes. God crossed my eyes but strengthened my ears. It is a curse. People stare at you and will never lead on that they are completely horrified and amused by your deformity. As a result, any conversation you have with a person is doomed to be filled with silences (and uncomfortable ones at that) because anyone with whom you speak is thinking, ah, he is cross-eyed, he must be like Jerry Lewis.

I see things you will never see, for crossed eyes are more focused. Laugh at me if you can find me. Most of the time I go out at night with sunglasses. I hate when people stare at me. To be honest I am suspicious of you, reader, for being so interested in my life. Anyone who reads has to be tired of his own existence.

I have never known what is customarily referred to as "love", yet I have experienced derivatives of it here and there and have seen various couples in the inane act, so I am somewhat familiar with the demesne. And I prefer to peep into the lives others rather than wreck my own. Vicarious pleasure allows you to get all hot and bothered. Let's face it, you can't give yourself a disease unless you're talking about depression, and that's another story.

Sometimes at night I like to take my tennis racket outside, find large roaches and whack them like I'm at Wimbledon. If I don't make this forehand, I will soon lose my new sports car, for as you know, once you succeed at anything, it becomes a matter of holding onto your money with dignity. It is requisite that you garner a wife. You then must place her in a cage, also known as a "nice house", and get her to pump out a few kids and not mind if one or two of them is resultant of the milkman or the cable connector. You pay to maintain this world, fall out of love and watch as your children descend into hatred for themselves, torturing their own genitalia or catching the cat on fire with a hearty chuckle or playing darts with Mommy's hind side.

In near death, I certainly had not forgotten about You. I imagine You above me, behind me, under my feet. Do You really listen to me? Have You any will of Your own or do You simply monitor the wills? I seem to have none myself. I seem to have lost myself long ago, to have forgotten what I learned, to have ignored it when I remembered. It is my opinion that You are oxygen to everyone but me. I see like You—are Your eyes crossed? I imagine You to be invisible to everyone.

Right now, I need something, and it is not a sign or grace or anything like that. My focus, though, is errant. I believe I am sick. Yesterday, I prayed to You. I am afraid to ask You for anything because I don't feel like I deserve it. I have shelter and food, enough at least to keep the skin covering my body. And books, I have them.

To have too much is to sink with weight into the soft ground. A big house full of stuff sinks faster than a small one full of nothing. And in a room of nothing one must also be nothing. Would You agree? You don't. You think I should stop inventing excuses to avoid getting a job. Well, I'm not getting one. You can forget it.

All of You are alike. You think just because I pray to You that You can manipulate me like a fool. I know I'm nobody and that is what I want to be, surrounded by nothing, not even You.

I need no one.

No, I don't. I don't. I'm not arguing with You anymore. We are not so dissimilar because You have a stalker, the devil. And I *am* a stalker. I will stalk You if I have to. Just because You're You doesn't mean I won't follow You. Wait, isn't to follow You the be-all of stalking training? To stalk the almighty You. Hmmm. How would one go about that anyway since You are invisible? I mean, nobody has ever seen You; they just talk about You. How is that even possible, to never be seen and still somehow exist? It makes no reasonable sense. You are only an imagined mountebank. I couldn't stalk You if I tried. Where would I find You? Just because of Your fabrication, I am going to reduce Your name from the majuscule (You) to the minuscule (you). From now on, You are you. If I ever see you, I will give you back your You. I doubt I will see you anytime soon.

BACK TO THE DESERT

There was nothing left for me to do except return to the place in the desert with the Joshua Trees. Out of Los Angeles a little over two hours near all those windmills, I stopped again. I had left in the morning and there was still daylight when I arrived. The desert floor was barren, nothing but miles of yellow dirt and cacti. And those windmills. I stopped my stolen car on the side of the road this time (instead of the middle) and stared at them spinning in unison, the visible propellers of invisible airplanes, hovering in space. The revolving hubs spun slowly and I could see the blades turn. In other places I could them spinning quickly, the mirage of a fan at its highest speed. I had not seen a single car on my drive out. Not one. I watched the windmills until an inky darkness filled the night.

Heading north on 62 I saw a tavern shaped like a large shoe box. Its architecture—well, I wouldn't go that far. The place reminded me of a trailer, only larger. There was an incomplete yellow neon sign pulsing OP-N in the only window. After I parked my car and rubbed my eyes, I stood on the soft dirt, slammed my door and made my way into the establishment. Several drunk people poured out like lemonade without the sugar added.

Inside, I deigned to scan the place. All the women dressed in a fashion from another time and all of the men looked like terrorists with moustaches who beat their children.

I took a seat at the bar, ordered a whiskey.

What kind? barkeep grunted.

Uh, nothing clear-colored. Only orange. Yes, orange whiskey.

He tilted his head back as if he were trying to cross his eyes and gander at his nose hairs and continued this action for many moments.

Orange whiskey, I repeated, ignoring that he made fun of me. Ahm . . . yeeeaah.

After many minutes nothing was poured. I waited. At a table for two in the corner was a blond couple arguing. Both stood out like ripe apples on a tree of rotten, bruised fruit.

And when you get a chance, barman, send two orange whiskeys to my new friends over there.

I don't think he heard me. Why do they keep the music so loud in these places? Bunch of vociferating magpies. After thirty minutes I gave up on the whiskey and decided to see who the people were at the corner table. They appeared to be actors. Now, I don't know if you ever notice, but soap opera actors are extremely good-looking. However, film actors are almost always short, ugly and have acne.

I was certain that I recognized the lady from the screen. Her face was a strawberry with a narrow chin, wide cheekbones, wider forehead. She was humble and sweet in her roles. Moving closer to her and her boyfriend, however, I noticed "pustules" on her face. The two of them were striking but not really beautiful. They were annoyed to be noticed, likely bothered that they would never be as pretty in person as they were in films. But something about them was appetizing, and I decided I would have them both by the end of the evening. I sat at a nearby table and listened to him try to assuage her fear about a woman friend of his. He kept telling her not to worry. While he put his hand on hers, he also suggested that she not drink anymore, due to adverse affects it might have when combined with her numerous medications.

With that, she rose quickly and yelled, Well, why did you bring me to the bar then? Her hand came down hard on the table splashing drinks in his lap. He wiped what he could off himself and seemed hardly bothered.

Why don't you have a soda instead of that liquor? he suggested. A nice ginger ale, hm?

She slammed her hand on the table again. Thank goodness it was loud enough elsewhere to not draw any attention to the commotion.

My medicine, she challenged, and remained standing, has nothing to do with how I'm acting. You. You are the problem.

I'm not the one who spits on people.

Shut up.

And socks them in the face and is unable to remember doing so the next morning.

That has nothing to do—

She was almost ready to cry.

And sabotages a person's work and laughs about it.

I didn't mean to, she said, more humble now.

And leaves scars on my arm from scratches.

Stop.

And pummels her own face ten times in a row.

Stop. She sat down.

I have never met anyone as irresponsible for her actions as you.

She said nothing.

If I had done one-tenth of the cruel things you have done to me, he said. One-*tenth*.

He held his thumb and forefinger very closely together, right in front of her face. She jutted out her chin.

What? she challenged. *What*? Finish.

You would be pulverized.

Such a pussy, she said.

For not hitting her back, he said, looking over at me, I am, hence, a pussy.

Such a Christian! she shrieked.

I forgive you for all the things you've done to me. And I will forgive you if you do them again.

Christ. I'm dating Christ.

I won't hurt you, he repeated. Ever.

You really know how to make someone feel bad.

I love you more than you can accept. One day, you'll be thankful. One day.

Oooh, you make me so sick.

Why don't you let me give you a big hug? he asked.

No.

He touched her neck with the back of his hand. Just at the moment I thought she might acquiesce to kindness, she ran from the bar as he gazed at her and shook his head, displaying an insouciance so blithe and impressive I had to admire him for a moment. He was like a farmer who has lost ten cows in a hurricane and stands in the field near their bodies, stoic, almost amused, worried more about whether or not he has paid the phone bill or if there will be enough peanut butter for his sandwich at lunch.

Meanwhile, she was knocking over chairs, spilling beers on an empty table and kicking the door open.

The man placed some bills on the table and nodded at me. I was sitting near him. He stood and stretched. I must have been staring impolitely. He was not bothered. In fact, after he inhaled a few times and stretched his neck to both sides, his eyes caught mine and in what I think has to possibly be the saddest single moment in my life, the threat of futility reddened his face. Tossing his head in the direction where the woman had blazed a path, he stared. After he put his hands in his pockets, he nodded to me.

It is a criminal offense to burn the Joshua Tree, thereby sending me to an old construction site where I broke some boards with the heel of my foot and put them in my sporty car. Make a mental note to speed very fast, I told myself, and drove to the Joshua Trees. Suddenly, I careened around a corner and glanced at the speedometer and realized I was going almost a hundred miles an hour. I sped up and rolled down all the windows. The night breeze was almost cold, and I thought how brisk life could be at times.

When I remembered I had stolen the car, though, I slowed down and noted the quietness around me. No insects even chirped. Arid, absent of arable soil, desolate, barren, the desert reminded me of myself. There is only sparse vegetation within me. I have never flourished. I am so dry that I have forgotten what water tastes like—it has a taste, you know. Not a flavor. A taste.

A few hours must have passed before I parked the car at a vacant campsite (most of them were not occupied) and went for a walk to look for a spot to sleep. Instead of making two trips, I loaded the wood from the trunk onto my arms and hiked among the small mesas and thousands of trees that look like well-fed cacti. On a flat plane I dropped the wood, pulled out some newspaper from my back pocket and proceeded to make a fire. I could not light it and decided to just go to sleep.

On the brink of slumber, I heard an awful scream in the distance. I listened and heard it again and roused myself and ambled through the trees and tried to locate the voice.

Hello? I tried, not very loudly, afraid to disturb the night.

I was still in the middle of sleep, not knowing who I was or why I was where I was or what this noise could be.

It was a tent. A light glowed translucent through the green material like a lightning bug's belly.

I heard a man's voice: I'll speak to you all night.

The quiet, she whispered to him. I don't like the silence.

No need to scream anymore. I'm here.

I listened. Her shivering teeth cut the cold night air. I actually heard her teeth chatter.

I love you, he whispered.

The couple from the tavern?

A wind rustled some trash on the asphalt. They had barely set up their tent on the desert itself, staying close the camp site.

Do you love *me*? he asked.

She wanted to scream again. I don't know how I knew, but I did.

There is someone stalking us, she fussed. Somebody's following us.

I don't think so, he told her. I don't think so.

She would not say she loved him. He did not ask her anymore. I listened for a long time. Finally, I left them alone. Poor people. My pity for them broke my heart in half.

I do not know if you understand my life and what it means to have no one, knowing they have all given up on you. Some see you as too intense while others think you are too depressed. Since you refuse to work and waste your life in the meniality of that fatuous thing known as a job, you have no money either. You own nothing because possession is sinful and heavy. You walk by yourself and the world avoids you due the scowl on your face that you have no idea you're wearing, until you look in the mirror one sad night in the middle of your life and see that you are unhappy and you want companionship, but you have spent so much time avoiding it that you know it will never be yours.

When you go home, you go home by yourself, walking with nobody's arm looped through yours. Your apartment is solitary. There is no furniture and rarely is food available. Will you change, you ask yourself sometimes, and you answer no, no I will not. I will not, not because I won't, but . . . and then you stop. You look around. You notice your freedom from pettiness. You are able to see everything as it should be. Perspective is what you have; it is your gift, the sole one. It is your talent. You cannot multiply your insight: it remains constant like zero. All things multiplied by zero are still zero. Nothing times anything is nothing.

Amid stone hills I woke up the next morning to tan, purple, sage, yucca, gray. I stretched the ache from my bones and tendons. One side of my body had a deep chill because wet dirt had found its way under my skin. Since there were no tall trees to give shade, the light was fierce and metallic and caused me to squint and hold my hand over my eyes to see. Why had I not brought any water? Because I was not leaving, that's why. I wanted to dry up and blow away in the Joshua Trees. I had reached my acme of stalking You (now you). It was my apotheosis. There was nothing left to stalk. I was going through the stalking motions, following people with no purpose. I didn't even know why I was here.

My shins smarted. When I looked down at my feet, I noticed a green ball of needles, much like an elaborate pin cushion, stuck on my shoe. Then I noticed three others on my legs. Reaching down, I very carefully pulled them off one by one. I soon realized the small cacti had barbs at the end of their spindles, so that they actually curved into my jeans and boots and one into the back of my calf. I had to move slow, and even after I had finished, I had cactus splinters in my fingertips. They seemed embedded and I could do nothing about them until I found a knife somewhere.

It mattered none, for I had decided to blend into the desert. Perhaps I was becoming a cactus. I imagined that I was a sandstorm eddying through the rocks, lacerating stones and anything else in my wake with small grains of myself. I imagined I was a Joshua Tree and stood still and waited to become one. I walked deep into the desert and saw no one. Since I wanted no water, I was never thirsty, and since I feared no hunger, I required no food. My feet were blistered, my fingertips burning from the jumping cholla cactus splinters.

I walked away. Maybe I would hear a voice to compel me back to the person I used to be. Maybe out in the open, forsaking my body, I might just hear that voice. I might be beckoned to an important task. I might *matter*. I prayed for a vision.

The afternoon passed like a bored turtle. I stared directly into the sun in the middle of the day and I was not afraid to be blind. I stared. Ah! The sun! I had not stalked the **sun**. My eyes were wide open. They teared but they were not tears. I saw blemishes of light and redness and still I kept them open. And just when I was about to lose my sight forever, just when I was about to be blessed with a recognition, a malady, a distinction, I heard her again. I turned to see them both in my blurriness. She had an ax like Kitty with her bat and was chopping down a Joshua Tree as he begged her to stop. My vision was full of smudges.

I ran to them and asked them to help me. I told them that I needed water for my eyes. I had stared at the sun for a long time and it had not fully blinded me, but now I needed water. I saw the ax chopping. My eyesight became lucid for one second and in another I saw nothing but ink. I saw that it was not an ax but a camera on a leather strap. She was angry, whipping the tree.

It's not a real tree! she screamed. This place doesn't make sense.

I could still see the large formation of rocks that weren't quite mountains or mesas, just monolithic piles of stone. I could see the sky and henna colored stones and the arms of all the Joshua Trees. I could see a small dirt road. Even though I saw what the desert contained, more than anything I saw emptiness. The space I saw was empty.

They are called Joshua Trees, he said. When the Mormons came into the desert, they thought the trees were the arms of Joshua welcoming them into the promised land.

This, and she pointed to the one she had been hitting, looks like a cactus. Nothing like a tree. She whacked it some more.

He gave no answer.

Doesn't it look like a cactus? She might have speaking to me.

If you could, he begged, if you could just tell me when you are going to be like this, I would apprecia—

Like what! she screamed. Like what?

Can't you see we have company? Ha. Company. That's funny. We have company.

I might go blind, I informed them. I've finally seen the sun. Lived all my life and it's been right there and I've never really taken the time to look at it. The sun is not so easy to follow, but you *can* stalk it. For a moment. Oh, you *can*.

See, the man spoke, we even a have prophet here. He is challenging God. He has looked into the sun.

My eyes hurt very much, I admitted. In my head I cry. But my eyes burn. They burn.

This freak, she challenged. Ha. He was in the bar last night. And I'll bet you that was him breathing heavy outside our tent last night.

My head swam. I swooned. I fell and knew that what hit my head was a rock, that my head had split open and bled.

Leave him, she hissed.

No, I want to stay.

Leave him! she repeated.

He needs somebody to help him.

And I don't?

My hearing faded.

I have to stay. I have to matter to someone. I don't matter to you.

But—

Leave me here, he sighed. I have tried to matter to you.

But—

Please leave me alone. I will never think badly of you.

Whether she left at that moment, I don't know because I was blind again. When my eyes opened, my head pressed something soft, his shirt I assumed. I could only see blurs.

Eat this chocolate, he said, placing a melted chunk in my mouth. I chewed the sweet bitterness.

Why did you stare so long at the sun? he wanted to know.

I have no one, I said. I have little to give and I want to stop seeing myself in the mirror.

That's too bad.

Yet I am afraid to die. I almost died recently. I just couldn't make it happen.

Perhaps, he said, handing me another morsel of chocolate, you need a friend.

The night came faster. I couldn't budge. The darkness was a comfort.

He remained with me.

In the morning we stayed where we were.

Occasionally we smiled at each other.

I saw leopard spots and bubbles.

Another evening came.

Another relentless morning arrived.

We watched each other and did not speak.

Soon the days were a week.

She did not come back.

We weakened but we smiled. After ten days, I rose and helped him up and shook his hand and thanked him for sitting through my rough days with me. In the middle of the desert we parted, my sight much better.

After the desert I decided it was necessary for me to become an overachiever, but the difficulty came in figuring out how I would distinguish myself. Just when I created the resolve, I fell sick, violently ill, depressed and feverish. I stayed in my bed (the alley) wearing sweatpants, a sweater, wool socks and a wool hat. I was angry, my fever like a sunburn. I kept layering clothes on top of me to try and sweat out my malady. I was frantic and the only thing that compelled me was my writing. Summoning up the energy to do that was like a cripple grabbing for his crutches on a cold, early morning.

For one bright afternoon I stumbled around the city telling the bums I had nothing for them and apologizing for my own poverty. I walked through the back streets of Hollywood and never saw anyone like me, only suspicious but indifferent eyes darting my way. Around El Centro I headed north, wishing for a purpose while knowing that to stroll was the only thing I could really do at the moment. I couldn't afford to eat and wasn't hungry enough to beg. Fishing around my pockets I found a five-dollar bill! I couldn't believe it. I put it in my mouth and chewed but took it out because it made me sick.

Around Santa Monica Boulevard I hung a left and had to listen to the swarm of traffic when I stepped back onto the busy street. I saw no other walkers and passed by a few people waiting for the bus. They examined me as if I were a succulent face carbuncle. Deciding to move one street south, I crossed the asphalt and went through a neighborhood, passing by a young girl embosked within a leafless rose bush.

Hi, she said, shrugging at her poor cover. I know you can see me.

I hastened my pace, disembarrassing myself from her. Children scared me with their littleness. Nobody should be that little. I have never stalked a child. Only eighteen and over.

I hated the street south of Santa Monica and therefore returned to the busier boulevard and the staring, silent people.

All of you were returning to me. I was ready for you again.

Outside the supermarket you stood on the sidewalk beside a shopping cart. A very tanned face, so brown to almost be tomato red, is what I noticed first about you. In your shopping cart sat an old manila valise and a garbage bag of clothes. My chest was weak. I wore a black turtleneck and a long wool cardigan sweater to my knees. You showed your concern for my cold, although you refused to believe someone like me could fall ill.

You have bright eyes, you noted.

What did you mean? You did not insult my crossed eyes.

You asked me why I wanted to go into the store. I told you that I became very lonely when I wrote. You asked me if I earned money with my writing and I lied and said yes, which caused you to doubt me even more, for if I made money, why didn't I have any for you? Your hair was frizzy and abundant like an electrified voodoo doll, matting in places. Was it a wig? Your teeth were crooked and thin like a child's. You wore shorts, even though the night would soon be freezing.

Do you want some, ahm, what is the stuff I'm talking about? Come here.

I followed you the few feet to your cart. You dug into a wide pocket of your faux leather valise and pulled out two pills.

Yours, you offered. Ginseng.

Thanks.

I gulped the pills down sans water.

I have to get off welfare. I used to live in a building downtown—do you know what a hit parade is?

I did not. I sure knew a non-sequitur though.

Well, a hit parade, ahm—see, I lived downtown and there were a lot of people who smoke crack. A lot. All around me. And I don't know if they're after me, or what. Every time I came home, my roommate—I think he was in on it. Excuse my bad breath.

You paused to reflect for a moment, reached into the garbage bag and pulled out a tube of half-used toothpaste. After putting it into your mouth, you squeezed out a six-inch segment like a cat evacuating feces and licked it off. Before putting it away, you had the courtesy to offer me some. I informed you I had brushed my teeth yesterday and was fine on that account. You shrugged and continued your disjointed, albeit moderate tirade.

See, I came home every night and these guys were in the lobby. You know what the orange mafia is?

I said I didn't, knowing full well that *no one* knew what the orange mafia was.

Well, anyway, I came home every night, and I'm clean, I'm on parole, you know, I murdered a gerbil when I was a kid, but I know my roommate was in on it.

I nodded and waited for some sort of direction in your words. You spoke like a labyrinth with no minotaur in the center.

Do you know what minimal cyanide poisoning is?

No, I'm afraid I—

Say, your eyes are so bright. You're not really sick.

I told you I truly was.

Well, you said, take the ginseng.

I just did. I already took them.

Oh.

Chill crept around my neck and I informed you that I needed to go. You liked my turtleneck. I thanked you for the compliment.

Do you think you were poisoned? I asked, curious.

Well, cyanide kills you? Right? But whoever put it in my food or whatever—see, if you eat french fries then Jesus won't let the cyanide explode your stomach because that's what it does, it explodes your stomach and you die. But I think . . .

I realized you were now talking to the next person who also had a shopping cart. Using this new face as an excuse to dismiss myself, I bowed my head slightly, shook your hand and went to bed wondering if you found a place to sleep during the night.

No one knows me. No one knows what I am. I'm not stalking much these days. Writing is a form of clandestine stalking. Sometimes I labor in the quiet of the night or in the din of the morning. Ten hours, twelve hours, some days even twenty hours, I write. I chase words, but there are so many. The dictionary is galactic, words its particulates. I cede to this lexicon, for I cannot keep up with an infinity. Perhaps I should realize the same about following people.

Yes, I have a difficult time when I step out of my room. I do not know how to take care of myself. I barely need to eat and I certainly want no money. I want to be left alone but can't leave others be. This is my choice. But there are times when I need for you to know that my solitude is not for me but you. I am alone for you and when I am finished making my words, you can have them. They are yours. They were only mine briefly.

Do you know that I need you?

I hide from you because I exploit you.

Because I had a fever, I wore a yellow and blue stocking cap and several shirts and two sweaters. There was a glow in the laundromat so intense as to be brilliant. My eyes strained to look at so many white machines gyrating. I gazed around at the see-through glass of the dryers with clothes spinning. I guess I reveled in the purity of soap and its impetus to make garments so clean, always clean.

Warm as it was, my body yielded to sopor and my eyes blurred. Some children frolicked, not thinking, not able to sit still. I felt sorry for them; they didn't appear to use their brains for anything more than motor coordination. At the moment before I nearly fell unconscious, I saw the boy in the basket being wheeled around by the girl. The basket tipped. I saw a nose coated with blood and the boy crying and you, his mother, running to him, comforting him.

My clothes dried. I folded them alone, placing them in a navy sheet and throwing it across my back like Santa. Those children caused me to think of you and the pond and the meals you used to bring me. Remember how we watched the mule deer eat oranges on the trees at night? And that time I saw a spider in mid-air as if suspended by nothing? Do you remember when the boy could not sleep? Because he had misbehaved, you took his radio and video games. You even took his t.v. He needed noise to rest. You yelled at him and pleaded with him to sleep. He was scared. I talked to him.

I can't sleep is why, he said to me.

Are you sad? I asked.

He said no. A tear quivered in the small red triangle of his eye.

Will you, I said, try to sleep in the quiet tonight?

It was cornea-singeing in the room. I asked him if I could turn down the lamp.

Do you remember all this? You should. You watched me from the door and smiled, your arms crossed.

Will you try the silence for me? I asked again. I rubbed his hair.

Soon he was asleep.

I switched the makeshift bag of laundry from one shoulder to the other, setting down the heavy pile for a moment. I tried to tie the bundle in different ways, but it was cumbersome and I had to force myself to make forward steps. Fortuitously, I found a shopping cart, placed the bundled inside and scraped away a peppering of ants. This lessening of my load allowed me to ride like I was on a big skateboard. The noise of the wheels cut the night. At one point I stopped and the silence was so severe that I heard no one. Nothing.

I wished for a hill and found one where Sunset intersects with San Vicente. I had no food and my shoulders and neck ached. I was cold and by myself. And there was the hill. Down I went. The cart careened to the left and right. I toppled sideways, scarring my thighs and back, and slid down the asphalt. My laundry remained intact. Without even noticing my blood, I righted the cart and finished the hill. Zoom. What a ride! I couldn't stop sailing despite warm blood dripping from my crash wounds.

At home I emptied the cart and went inside the house full of roaches. Before I could open my door and put away my laundry, the insane old man down the hall, the other squatter in the tenement, i.e. you, groped against the walls saying my name.

Is that you? you asked.

It is I, I said.

Ah, yes, you. You held up your finger.

Like a fountain spurting murky water, your epithets flooded over me.

You have made me sick! you screamed. I am dying in there. You have given me pneumonia.

Maintaining as much aplomb as I could, I accepted your enmity and did not recapitulate it your way. I was your apologist. For this reason, you should be thankful. You inquired if I knew of any places where you might purchase a monkey in exchange for seven remote controls you had found. Next, you scalded me verbally for my lack of knowledge about monkeys.

I wanted grab a hank of your hair. In my imagination I was a Cheechako in the Pacific Northwest a hundred years ago using my tomahawk to slice away your scalp. Instead, I fell below myself, morally, and called you a roundworm that infests intestines.

Nematode! I scolded you. Do *not* talk to me in this way.

This only riled you even more. I paused for a philosophical moment. What if you were a djinn sent here to micturate on my quasi-quiescent fairground? If so, then I was pinioned and needed to regroup and continue to listen to you, for I knew of the djinn. It was paramount for me to jugulate my evil urge to spew rejoinder.

You are a senile old man, a djinn in disguise, testing me, examining my quiddity and arraigning me for any ethical failures.

Well, I have you euchred because I know your game. Normally, insult operates on quid pro quo, unless one person chooses to be laconic and to watch, not reply. And that is what I am doing right now. I am thinking, not replying. Yes, you are a nematode. Ha, ha, you are a nematode. But while I am cogitating this fact, you have already perorated at great length as to how I have all but given you leprosy. I am, in short, the better man.

I have waited for this moment for a long time. And I am prepared. See, I sit at home and read and learn about what is right and then I attempt to maintain these credos. I have created a hospice within myself where the errant pilgrims of folly may rest. This imaret makes up my soul. Even though I have been ready, I still slipped because you caught me at the wrong time. I'm sorry for the nematode thing.

You can prepare yourself incessantly, but there is always something in you that will fail when the test comes. While you coarsely hurt me and accuse me, I will dream of eiderdown and moths playing against lampshades in felicity.

I am still listening to you. My smile increases.

Is it spurious to think you are wrong and allow you to continue your mouth-lashing while, in my mind, I want to respond to each vituperative barb? Your harangue is a painful decorticating. In a moment your peroration will cease and you will dissipate. Soon, I will hock an oyster of sputum from deep within my esophagus and spit it fiercely into the toilet, right in there with the ordure where it belongs. That spit keeps me from reacting to you. As you see, I am evolved beyond you. Goodbye. I am going to shut my door quietly now. Okay. Nice talking to you.

Bastard! you screaked. (Yes, screak is a word.)

Hey, I'm real sorry for calling you a nematode.

I have pneumonia, you cried, grasping at your scarf. You have made me sick.

You don't mean it, I calmly said.

I touched you. And walked you to your door. You thanked me.

Be strong, you offered.

Thank you.

I am not a bad man, you said.

Yes, I replied. I know.

I am okay now. I'm sorry for my yelling. I can't help myself sometimes. I am not myself today.

Now, you were fine. I said good night.

In my room I broke the mirror with my forehead. I would be fine later, I thought, as I stacked my laundry in piles on the floor.

WHO'S BETTER THAN YOU?

I needed a hobby and went to the park every day and tried to do back handsprings from a complete standstill. I attempted this gymnastic for a week or more. Needless to say, I banged my head every single time, for as we all know, it is necessary to perform what is customarily known as a roundoff, which entails a running start to allow you the velocity to flip backward. The roundoff is sort of a glorified cartwheel.

By standing still and lunging backward without any momentum, though, I nearly gave myself about seven concussions, landing flat on the back of my cranium every time. People gathering around me thought I was some sort of clown.

I was at a random park in the outfield of the baseball diamond. Nearby stood a black wooden gazebo like a daddy-longlegs. A bevy of mexican families sat comatose at the picnic tables gnawing on sandwiches and chicken legs, chewing with such indifference they could have been pre-slaughtered bovine. They watched me and nudged each other at the spectacle.

I stayed in center field for about four hours. These two women stopped and said they hadn't laughed so hard in their lives, that they had been watching me from the tennis courts up on the hill. And was I a comedian?

No, I informed them, I want to do a back flip, *no* roundoff.

Ha, ha, ha, they whinnied, like I was the funniest thing they'd ever seen.

Just to spite them I raised my hands over my head, peered behind me with my eyes strained to the side to see where the ground was, and amid the hoohawing, my legs flew up in the air right as my palms connected with the ground, jolting my shoulder sockets.

There I was standing on my head. I caught myself. Sure, I didn't flip all the way over, but I caught myself!

Upon righting my body and touching the soft bruises all over my scalp, I was satisfied with my accomplishment. Those two women gyrated on the ground like a couple of fireworks, crying with laughter. All right, that's enough, I wanted to say. Instead, I waved my hand at them and went back to business. The next attempt was not so great. I wish I had quit while ahead.

The minute I positioned myself and tilted back my head with a rapid lunge, the rest of my body ignored the signals I sent to it, and my legs remained firmly planted in the soft soil of the field. And so, upright as a rood, I fell backward beyond my will and landed on my back.

Luckily the ground was pliable. The issue was not pain here. Obviously not. Christ, I had just thwacked my head forty to fifty times. I cared nothing about the bruises I felt or the stars I saw. I just wanted to back flip from a standstill.

As I lay looking at the sky and waiting for the night, I watched the giggling ladies leave practically tripping each other. I stayed there for a while wondering what possessed me to be a fool, even though I knew I never felt like one until measured by the barometer of others. Faith must always be contingent on nothing but what is in you. Faith preempts the scorn of others. It puts you on your dais unabashed and proud.

Moisture seeped through my shirt. It was time to go. My body creaked when I came to my knees. Any pressure on my lower back brought tears to my eyes, and I could not move my neck from side to side.

I journeyed throughout the city the next day. Like Roland, the paladin, cousin to Charlemagne, I summoned all my moxie, which was hard, believe me, with my immobile neck. What was the object I needed, the icon that would metamorphose my prowess into its own quintessence? Divine beings are increated; they aren't made from anything because they simply begin to exist. I would find the divine in me. If I found the right item, I would transcend the derision of others. Down the filthy sidewalks through this quadrant and that one, I jumped over hydrants.

Writing, I realized, was self-stalking, a misnomer since true stalking was magnanimous, about others. I had already been a self-stalker and we all know how *that* went. Perhaps my stalking days were at an end.

Finally, I saw it in the window. It was an unbelievable vision. I stared at it for almost ten minutes admiring the shape and significance. Notwithstanding the patina of grease on the window, I saw luxurious glitter like millions of bright green sand grains.

Inside, I informed the clerk what I wanted. He carefully removed it from the spot. I paid him and he could see my pride. Outside, I put on the helmet, slipping it over my ears and buckling it under my chin.

I saw your faces and smirks as you came closer. I tried to ignore you. My strut became a run and then a sprint. I turned the corner at 3rd and hustled to the park where I was a little safer. You pointed at me and thought I was hilarious.

There was no way I was going to remove the helmet. Never. Inside, my bruises were protected. I heard less. The green helmet was a womb for my thoughts.

I ran to a field and stood for a moment. With sudden force I flipped backward. When I landed on my head, the helmet cushioned the fall. Nothing scared me now. *I would not take off this helmet.* I moved over to a sidewalk to test if it would still work.

Watch this, I thought, and did a series of back handsprings, kerplunking on the sidewalk each time my head thumped the concrete. A mass of people surrounded me. More laughing and shouted execrations. I felt sad for you. I was too exhausted to continue and moved from the sidewalk to the grass, sitting with my knees pulled to my chest, craughing (crying and laughing at the same time). I heard nothing in my helmet. All sound was muffled.

I found a ride to nowhere in the back of a truck with four taciturn mexicans. They stared at my helmet. A window opened into the cab and I heard a singer on a spanish radio station who sounded like a jackhammer repeating *mamacita* 612 times (I counted). And I hadn't even heard the whole song. Wind ripped past us. I-5 became the 101 Freeway.

Downtown, I hopped off and caught a bus to the Tar Pits. Now, you are only a shadow of yourself, the darkest possible, yet you seem proud of your darkness. If you find your light one morning, I hope you will remember that your inner voice led you there. I pray that you will keep your thisness, your haecceity. Remember the essence of this moment. It is important. It is stronger than any persona you can fake.

Just when I thought I would never see you again, there you were in the grocery with your three children! We acted like neighbors, friendly but full of boundaries. The boy wanted to hug me, but he was embracing a box of crisped rice cereal. Both girls looked strange and occupied. One of them asked me why I wore a helmet. You seemed gloomy, almost saturnine. I wanted to be with you again as the shock of our meeting circuited through me. In our conversation in the meat aisle, you said that a babysitter was picking up the kids soon for a movie, hinting that the house would be empty later. I understood your meaning.

I pushed my shopping cart over the asphalt intent with purpose. I passed under swaying trees and smelled the azaleas of my youth. Two raccoons ensconced in a magnolia stared at me, tilting their heads quizzically. The cart rumbled and banged from block to block until I stopped in front of your house. Clever of me to still have a key, I reflected, nodding approval to myself. I parked the small vehicle, opened the door and entered. I had some time before you arrived.

For some reason I went to the living room, pushed plants out of the way, dragged the t.v. to the other side and opened windows for fresh air. I had begun to sweat. Once I had tipped the sofa onto its side and nearly smashed all the toes on one foot, I proceeded to drag your couch outside. For nearly forty minutes I attempted to maneuver this huge piece of furniture onto that shopping cart, but each time I did so, it fell over one side or tipped the cart sideways.

Damn, I repeated many times. But with Titan pluck and an ability to forgo antipathy for you (symbolized in the sofa), I squatted underneath the unruly colossus. Upon loading it on my back and helmet, I, in the next instant, placed it across the middle of the cart.

Unfortunately, a startling contretemps occurred.

The boy appeared from nowhere.

Followed minutes later by none other than YOU.

YOU?

Well, dip my testicles in heavy cream and squat me in a roomful of kittens.

You held the magazine you had once prevented me from acquiring. You said that you carried it with you wherever you went. Daily, you had promised to rectify our past at the newsstand by one day returning what you had stolen from me.

There we stood, you and I, the sofa in equipoise, straddling the supermarket buggy. I realized the boy looked almost exactly like you. I had never made the connection.

YOU live here??!

I was beside myself.

Bygones? you offered. I am sorry. I have never felt right about stabbing your arm.

How was jail? I asked, bemused, shocked, confounded.

Fine, fine, was there just a few months, you reassured me. And your stab wounds?

Healing, I told him.

I have come to see my wife. This is our house. Or was until I went to jail. I'm trying to make things right. Gave up the porn.

Wife? Did you say wife?

I have a wife. And a son. And two girls. They were just at the grocery store and I'm about to take them to a movie.

Yikes, I muttered.

It wasn't possible.

You were with YOU?

This is too much, I thought. Too much.

Before I forget, you added, here is your magazine. I found it in prison. All the prisoners liked it. They said the linear structure of the narrative propelled them beyond fetters of any existential bounds they had previously envisioned for themselves, and that in juxtaposing their imprisonment with the story of the girl who could vanish when abused, they were liberated within their own four walls to individuate.

They said all that? Multiple prisoners actually *said* that?

I'm sorry I prevented you from buying it that day. I regret it.

Ahhhh, no big deal, I said, shrugging. Nevertheless, I snatched the magazine from him.

Do you know my wife? you asked. What are you doing here?

Ye—um, no, I don't. I am just delivering this sofa to a client. And your wife is that, er, client. I am in the sofa scrubbing business now. Of cleaning off sofas by scrubbing them a lot with a new technology that is gentle to the environment; it's a scouring liquid made from purified goat-penis sweat. So here's your sofa! All clean and ready for your return home from jail.

The boy was about to expose who I was, then I think he realized how it might hurt you, his mother, so he stopped himself.

Er, why are you wearing a green helmet?

I'll be going, I announced, and burst into a sprint.

I have no idea why I wanted your sofa in the first place, but I guess it was somehow designed by You to get back my short story. I guess You can have Your majuscule You back again. I re-believe in You due to this abnormal serendipity.

You are married to YOU! Unbelievable!

Later that night, I helmetedly rode my bike on the sidewalk and was conscious of my space wanting no one around. I cursed people before I passed, laughing to myself about their faults afterwards. I neologized a portmanteau: bike + rage = bage. The bage was pervasive.

I pedaled my bike right inside a thrift store on Fairfax to peruse books. A little man with a flounder face remained in front of me. His lips, chapped to the point of peeling, protruded like a kiss.

Move, I mumbled, under my breath.

He shifted himself, his head tilted to the side. I biked past him.

I perused the shelf, found one used book called *The Reclusives* and was ready to go. Again, the homunculus stood in the doorway and wouldn't let me through with my bike. I noticed a lot of strange people staring and drooling. Then I biked down an alley to ease my mind.

My stalking journal, *YOU*, would be over soon and an encomiast would be pronouncing its eulogy.

YOU MUST DANCE

A rhapsody is an instrumental fantasia on folk songs. A rigadoon is a lively french dance. A saraband is a stately oriental or spanish dance. Vigoroso means what it seems to mean. And if you imagine of all of these dances done vigoroso and add to them a habanera, a cuban contradance, you will, perhaps, just maybe, have the feeling I'm having.

Editor, I just received your letter. I am in my tenement building hallway staring at the accompanying check. My story did not, after all, die in the little magazine. As an editor, you believed in me. Even though the smaller literary journal folded, my story is in a larger anthology read by thousands, possibly trillions. I can finally move from this tenement.

You, my senile neighbor, emerged and cavorted with me, telling me you no longer had pneumonia, saying how strange it was that I had once called you a nematode. We laughed about our past confrontative bobbery.

A polka! A samba! A tango! I backsprung up and down the tenement hallway, wearing my helmet which I always wore to bed. A scottish fling. A mazurka. A jarabe. A jaleo.

I realized I was naked too! A gavotte. A galop. A pavana. A minuet. A folia. And of course a fandango. Why not some break-dancing? Chaconne? Redowa?

A bergamask? That's the dance.

Yes a bergamask, the dance of clowns.

I kissed my check, my first. King of Editors, bless you for this check.

Too elated to speak, I clothed myself and ran outside to tackle the morning. After a few moments a strange feeling occurred. The sun was not to be seen and clouds covered the sky with mouse gray. And where were the people? I walked south on my street to

Wilshire hoping to see the bustle of cars and buses, but it was silent. And then it hit me. Morning. Early morning in the city and it was about to rain.

I had not noticed this matutinal time since I played basketball with you. I raised the check over my head and walked down Wilshire, west, toward the beach. I walked all morning, stopping once for coffee and a danish, passing the Tar Pits first, then Fairfax Avenue, into clean Beverly Hills, West Los Angeles and lastly Santa Monica. I came to Ocean and took a left and headed down the pier, found the stairs down to the bike path and arrived at the hanging rings, my hypnotic metal friends.

It was about ten o'clock and I saw no one but a bald female bouncing on a trampoline. I stepped on the platform, grabbed the first ring and thought of you and the milk on the floor with all those utensils, and how I wanted to scorch my insides with coffee on the way home. What was wrong with me then? I swung all the way to the end. Jollily, I hopped on the concrete path and made my way to Venice.

I passed the colorful shops, one of which offered iced-tea enemas. I went by the tiny little black man with no legs and a little nub for an arm. I listened to the blond guy with the sexual healing powers who breathed into the microphone like he was about to fellate it. I noticed a young hippie couple sculpting the erotic torso of a female from sand. I crossed over to where some skinny girls danced on rollerblades and rollerskates. At the basketball court I saw a fist fight between gang members. Onward to the rope.

Removing my shoes (and deciding to never return to them), I approached a pull-up bar feeling sand on my ankles. At the rope I stared straight up and nodded. Tired from the rings I readied myself.

I climbed.

I climbed with my legs parallel to the ground. Halfway up my stomach muscles gave out and I nearly dropped to the ground, but I held on tight and breathed. A group was below me.

You can do it!

I know, I thought.

I don't need you.

I have never needed you and I certainly don't now. I am up in the air. I touch the top. I see the ocean. I remain where I am. I am pleased. When I find my check in my back pocket, I hold it high, as high as I can. I knock on my helmet twice. Who's there? Oh, me. Kind of got excited there and forgot that I had knocked.

I descend. Slowly. Fist over fist, never sliding. I am in control. The check is in my mouth. I am barefoot. I run over the bike path, over a wall, onto the beach, toward the ocean. In the middle of the day, it is so hot I just want to lie down and absorb the sun's heat. On the warm sand, I fall asleep. The walk and the climb have made me tired. A yawn opens my mouth very wide. It will be a good sleep . . .

Dark when I open my eyes. The sand is cold again. My check is still in my pocket, I discover, reaching for it in a moment of paranoia. Where will I go now? I meander on the beach. The air feels so sweet and wet. I want to stay. I don't know what to do. I never know what to do.

YOU MUST GO

You are the city, I tell myself. It is your imprimatur for rage and exculpation. It is a pantheon of breath but with air that is effluvia, vapor that has no oxygen. You have been left by all, and yet everyone is still here. This is your stalking sine qua non. You stalk the city itself; it follows you closely in return.

Here, you fancy yourself the restive preternatural libertine. You walk down the sidewalk and see a man drinking in a building recess. You walk past him and he slams his bottle to the ground, intractably. You are docile. You hold it in. You act as if you don't mind his shattered glass when you truly do. You walk another block and a man is peeing. He waves to you. You must stand silent and stolid and concrete and not content. Anywhere in the city is your coign of vantage. The city mollycoddles you into speciousness. Fretting becomes bitterness.

You waited for the bus at an intersection. You were the only one for miles who carried a book with you. You read *The Reclusives* in the dimness of the bus stop. Messages were scraped into the wood of the bench with knives, curlicues of graffiti, yet another language you would never understand no matter how long you stared at it. You sat alone for a bit. Ten minutes passed. Others came. Cars stopped at the light and stared at you and wondered why you didn't have a car and what kind of person you must be for wearing a green helmet at a bus stop. You stared at them briefly, urban eyes passing.

Soon the book you read meant nothing. It was late and the bus only went on the hour. A man who smelled of drink and sweat was selling roses. He stumbled near you, afraid to ask you to buy one since you were beginning to wear your rage even more. Your eyes told him to stay away, to not even sit on the bench.

Thirty minutes passed and you thought you were about to cry. You looked at your book again and wondered why the words blurred. Too dark to read now. Your throat burned. Fifty minutes. You gritted your teeth. Tension under the back of your shoulder felt like Christ's palms being nailed. Your book lay beside you. An hour. An hour and ten. An hour and fourteen. The bus oozed along like a snail. You let everyone go before you, recompense for denying them the bench. You left your book behind. It had failed you.

On the bus you stood as the almost empty car swayed you from side to side. You wanted to inhale, but the air was so sour that you forgot about deep breaths. You stared at the bus driver's right elbow. You wondered about its pallor as compared to the rest of her henna body. The seven of you on the bus stared ahead. No one dared to speak for fear that the other might be friendly. Although people did not know why the talking had stopped, you definitely knew that it had.

Up La Brea, across 6th, over to 3rd, then to Beverly. At Beverly a sunburned man, displaced from some agrarian setting, attempted an ascent to the electronic fare taker. He had jackhammer arms and wore a sleeveless green t-shirt. He tried to slip his dollar in the slot. The annoyed driver waited. The man tried again. The bus driver tried to just grab the bill, but he pulled it away from her. Her foot depressed the gas in revenge. Determined, he squinted his eyes and aimed for the slot that pulled in the dollar. The bus jumped forward like a dragon hiccupping. The large man was felled and lay silent on his side.

The riders stared. You wondered if you shouldn't stand and help him. He remained on the bus floor until the next stop. The driver came to a halt, yanked the emergency brake, stood and grabbed him under the armpits. With a shove of the knee, she barreled him forward until he fell down the steps, his face smacking the sidewalk and causing numerous grimaces. A boarding passenger lifted one leg at a time and walked over him. Staring over her shoulder as she flashed her pass, she headed down the aisle to sell incense.

The driver crossed over Melrose still going up La Brea. She stopped here and there: Willoughby, Santa Monica, Fountain.

You decided to get off at Sunset where you crossed La Brea and sat at another bus stop. A drunk man sat beside you. His beer was in a bag and he offered you some. Eyes closed. Skin like the belly of a snake. A chinese man in a stocking cap. He could barely speak. You noticed that you were so filled with rage you were about to give up. The cars rolled by in an interminable parade.

You thought of you with your three children.

And you who kept me from buying my story at the newsstand. Out of jail now and home again.

You sat at the bus stop with the man who held his beer in a bag and listened to him.

In Janweery of 1556, in Sh-Shi. He burped. China! Dere was an earfquake that kilt 830,000 people. And you think *you* important?

He stabilized himself on the bench beside you, sipped his beer.

After a minute he passed out and fell asleep on your shoulder and you let him. You began to do what you hated and that is feel yourself. As the tears poured over your face like vomiting, you stood and gently cupped the man's head in your hands and placed him on the bench. You took off your jacket, for he wore no shirt, and covered him.

The next bus came.

You boarded again, going east, toward downtown, east on Sunset, past the smoggy ugliness, the anomie.

You stayed on until the end of the line, saying goodbye to the driver.

After walking down Cesar Chavez you turned on Alameda.

In the cathedral of Union Station you gazed at the very tall ceilings, pristine with aged wood. You bought a ticket for the train and walked down the warm tunnel to your boarding area.

Twenty minutes later on the train, sitting by yourself, you handed your ticket to the master.

The next morning you reached the north after long sleep and a dream about all of you, every one of you.

You woke up and got off and found a road and held out your thumb, but reconsidered, thinking you wanted no help from others, not because you wouldn't like a ride: you just, very simply, wanted to pull in your thumb.

The Ill-usives

street fiction

For David Kirkland,
gifted teacher

Do you have a daddy?
I'll bet you do.

—Eminem
"My Dad's Gone Crazy"
The Eminem Show, 2002

CHAPTER 1
The Stoop

Sometimes you not from the streets but you end up on em anyway. Eerybody call me Wig and I been tryin to make my life right for a long time. Seem like as much as I live, I nose-dive, can't find money to even get food sometimes, but I'm this albino, I mean, I ain't really albino, but I might as well be, what I mean is that, I'm *sick* of bein white, white people is some assholes! They uptight, they can't drive, they look at you funny, cut you down with them stares of theirs, you know what I mean too if you ever seen one of them starin at you. I can't say fuck white people tho cuz my dad was white.

And I'm white.

On the outside at least.

See, I was raised by a black mom and a white dad, but I never got one ounce of Momma's color, and I end up havin to tell black people that I really am black, even tho they don't believe that shit. I live in this place on Burnside in L.A., which ain't Compton, but it ain't Beverly Hills neither.

Okay, so last night, this freak Kit Fisher from downstairs knock on my door and I stare at him through the fishbowl eyehole and ax him what he wants, without openin (cuz you don't wanna open that shit around here, if you know what I mean).

He's, like, can I borrow your license?

Now, I know him, so I'm like, I guessss I'll open the door but he's wearin a mini-skirt and eyeliner and I'm just tryin to relax. I'm like, *pleeease.* My license? I ain't givin that to you! After I say no, I see him go next door and knock and ax the same thing!

Yeah, I say "ax" and talk black, whatever "black" is. Who made up what's black and white anyway? Get in my face about it. Please. I know who I am. Just seem like no one else does.

I'm half and half but I look like whole milk. Oh, hold up, half and half is white too!

Aw shit, Fooby comin. Fooby. Damn. I'm tryin to write down some shit about my long-ass day and Fooby always be around the corner. He a Blood and he gon wanna hide in my one-room studio. Through my window, I can see his ass runnin from about ten Crips, ha ha, chasin his ass. One night I ain't gon open my door, but I'll let him hide in here now.

Knock, knock.

"Hey Wig, is Foob. Open up."

When Foob about to get shot, he all, like, Wig is my friend, but that is some booooshit cuz he never come around otherwise, seewhatI'msayin? I let him in tho. Foob been shot about ten times but keep livin. Anybody get shot that much and still keep runnin, hey, I *got* to open my door just to have somma his luck-to-be-livin rub off on my ass. He gon wait for them Crips to pass, take a piss, prolly steal somma my Little Debbie cakes and leave.

This apartment buildin a bitch. It's all black, eerybody is black, except me and Kit Fisher (that crazy dress-wearin writer) and some mexican dude. Now I'm half-black but look whiter than an uncooked biscuit, but you woulda thought I was Hitler or some shit for livin here. And that rubs me wrong cuz Momma was blacker than all these bitches. Then when they find out I'm half-black, they think I'm some kinda booshitter, like I'm makin it up to have the pleasure of livin in this crack house. Shiiiit.

I ended up here cuz my flipped-out dad finally kicked me outta the house. So it's like I got all the whiteness from him on the outside but all the blackness inside from Momma. And I'm always tryin to prove to people that my inside is me, not my outside. When that fails, I have to back up and tell myself that I'm both my outside *and* my inside cuz you can't hide from things that made you. Ain't nobody helpin me along either. I just have to figure it out.

Meanwhile, Chester, the apartment manager, knocks on my door and axs for rent in his red robe that keeps "accidentally" fallin open. And when I give him a check, he's like, "Um, can I get halfa this in cash?" What, so you can get a rock to smoke? I ain't givin you cash for nothin.

Thank god for Mack C down the hallway. He famous on the streets for "Smash", this track eerybody knows. He lay down "Smash" and his crazy-ass wife be screamin up on the streets here sometimes, yellin up at his window. *Crash was, smash was.* You ain't heard it, you don't know it. "Smash". You prolly can't even find it now, but he scratched that shit on red vinyl. You never heard nothin like it.

So niggahs can't dismiss me.
Whiteys can't accept me.
Stuck. What the fuck.
Bein in the black middle,
white man's riddle,
extremes that frame my personality,
today, white one day, black the next,
talk it out, but
all the talkin
is just walkin outta
some chance to talk real.

Growin up, I was always gettin called the w-word, just cuz of the way I talk and the way I look.

"Why you talk black and look white, w——?"

"I wish you wouldn't call me that."

"Ha ha, w——!!!"

That's when I started headbuttin people. I got some hard head on me and they never called me w—— after that. Blacks and whites was callin me w——too.

Gettin it from all sides.

So I would get all these bruises on my white forehead, and it was about the only thing black on me. I think I kinda liked *lookin* black and kept on headbuttin to get more bruises. Which was real stupid,

I know, since now my head hurts like a bitch. As much as my heart stings from the namecallin. Momma said to ignore them people who use the w-word, but *how* can you dismiss that hateful shit?!

On top of gettin namecalled, now I'm all dizzy and pass out sometimes, just be walkin down the sidewalk and fall my shit over. Earlier today, I blacked out real hardcore. Hey, why ain't that shit called "whited out" cuz all I see is white when it happens? Hm. Maybe it should be a cross between white and black . . . whack!

Anyways, I blacked/whited out and when I opened my I's, I saw this thin African sister. And she was lookin into my I's and wipin blood off my face with a tissue and singin, "You gon be alright tonight, you gon be alright."

Man, I'm tellin you she was straight-up singin to me, cooin, and I just didn't even wanna talk for a long time so she wouldn't stop that little melody. Sister kept pullin tissues from her Michael Kors handbag and was just scrapin blood off my gushin forehead. Them bloody tissues was droppin onto the sidewalk while all the judgers in L.A. just kept walkin past, my sister cradlin me like Mary with Jesus in that statue, and *if you think I don't know about the Pietà, lemme throw what I know atcha.* See, I always got to prove I'm not stupid, but I even been to the Vatican bitch! I seen Pope John Paul II with my momma and daddy.

Let's break this down once and for all.

I *look* white.

I *sound* black.

Niggahs be hatin me and callin me the w-word.

Whiteys be hatin me and sayin I'm white trash.

Now, that's Monday.

On Tuesday, whiteys be callin me the w-word and niggahs say I'm white trash.

Fast-forward to Friday when niggahs be callin me the w-word *and* white trash **and** whiteys be callin me the w-word *and* white trash.

Got so many racists out there, black and white, wonder what name I be called tonite.

Man, I had to crack my head to fall in some love! After she wiped all the blood away, she helped me stand. *Once we were standin, oh man, I nearly dizzied down on the sidewalk again!* This sister was Mila. She said her name and leaned forward and kissed me on the right cheek.

"Now you alright," she sang real gentle in my ear.

I knew I had to get back to the apartment and clean up my sloppy self. I also knew Mila would never love me back and thanked her and began to walk back past La Brea Tar Pits, but she followed right behind me and caught up and walked beside me. We didn't say much and I was glad to be side-to-side.

I was ashamed to walk up to the buildin with all the crackheads on the stoop. There was this one supposed wife-beater, Crowner, who wore tight tanktops and had all kinds of tats. He lived on the stoop and was right there with five other guys when I walked up with Mila. I was expectin to have to be doin some more headbuttin with my bloody mess of a head, but you know what? Crowner smiled at me and just let me go by. "Wig, you get a pass, know I'm-sayin?"

"Thanks Crown." I did. I did know.

Now, it may not mean much to many, but that there pass was Martin Luther *King* to me. Crowner givin it to me was even truer. So that sealed him and me. After he gave me the pass, I grabbed Mila's hand and pulled her along into the buildin.

Once we came to my door, I was afraid, so many feelins in me. I didn't have much. I had been sleepin behind the Ralph's supermarket for the last month before I finally made some coin to rent here. And I was just happy to have a mattress and all my books. As we stood outside the door, I thought:

This is who I am
right now,
all I got,

*can't be worryin bout
what you think I'm not.*

I had one room with a small bathroom off to the side and a hot plate and a tiny brown fridge. But that shit was *mine*. At least I wasn't takin her back to the dumpster behind Ralph's! Mila walked in and went straight for the books. I didn't have no art. Books were my little Picassos.

"They call you Wig?" she said, lookin at Bernard Malamud's *The Tenants*.

"Yeah."

"Hm."

I have to admit I stared at my sister's ass right here. *Been resistin, tryin to listen to her mind, but I just took a glance at her tight behind.* I mean, let's break it down: tall African sister holdin one of my favorite novels in *my* crib. Damn.

"Where you get so many good books?"

"Poor man's book store: Goodwill."

"You got some music?"

"Yeah . . . yeah!"

Now, I still had an old cassette player and I put in old-school *Soultrane* by Coltrane. I think she was expectin some hip-hop when that Coltrane jazz was movin through us. We talked about books and my rich white dad who gave me nothin and how my black momma sounded like an English teacher but my blue-collar dad almost sounded black. People called him white trash cuz his daddy was a plumber. My dad worked in a chicken-processin factory, went to community college and played his trumpet whenever he could. He was involved in some bad shit now. That's why I left. He was gettin worse. Turnin into a monster. Made some money the wrong way and messed himself up with the wrong peeps. My momma worked for the government for the IRS. She was about the whitest black woman I ever met. My dad was the blackest white person I knew.

"You all confused then," she said, touchin my face.

Mila and I talked about books that whole afternoon. It was dark soon and I axed if I could walk her home.

"Maybe I am home," she said.

I thought she meant that she wanted to stay with me.

"I live here," she added. "Just upstairs."

"Oh! For *real*? I never saw you."

"Maybe you never looked," she teased me. "And anyways, I just moved in last week."

About that moment, I looked out my window up on the second floor, the same window where I could usually see Fooby comin to hide with me, and I saw this Hummer speedin up the street and aimin right for the buildin, the place where Crowner and his boys would stand on the stoop. I grabbed Mila's hand and rushed down the hall, down the stairs to see that s.u.v. drive into the yard and aim right at this drug dealer name of Berno. Berno walked with a cane and had been shot in the stomach once.

I see Fooby divin out off the stoop with all the others, except Berno who, I guess, knew it was comin. So there's Berno by hisself, high on crack. The door to the front was opened and I could see it happen, that tinted-glass comin like a killer wasp and the Hummer just rammin into Berno, his cane crackin, his knees bucklin, the truck reversin fast back to the street and drivin off.

Berno was flat on the stoop and eerybody came back to him like flies comin back to manure. We only had one phone in the buildin. I ran up to Mack C's room and he let me into the closet where he kept the phone. I called 911.

Back down at the stoop, they stood around Berno and I walked over to Mila and she clutched my hand again. Crowner came up to me and I told him the ambulance was comin. We waited with the body on the concrete steps. Mack C came down eventually and looked at Berno, shook his head and said, "Man, I told that niggah to stop doin that shit!"

When the ambulance came, we watched them roll him away. I looked down to see that there was no blood at all. They forgot his cane, so I picked it up and ran after them and put it beside him on the stretcher.

Eerybody went inside to they own rooms. Mila wanted me to see hers and I walked up another flight with her. Inside, she shut the door and leaned into me and her lips came to mine. She put on some Lil' Kim, "No Time", real quiet tho, and our hips was goin. Puff Daddy was doin his intro: "I got, no time for fake niggaz . . ." Then I heard Lil' Kim go, "Gotta hit the spot, if not don't test the poom poom . . ."

She turned down the music and wanted to talk.

"I can't call you Wig, it don't feel right," she told me. "What can I call you?"

"Benjamin," I said. "My name is Benjamin."

I made Mila leave. I mean, I was havin headaches still from my fall and needed to clean my ass up. Plus, I didn't wanna ruin that shit. Yeah, I wanted to *tap* that, but I also liked her. She was a kind sister and saw me for who I was. I had bigger things to deal with anyways. See, I'm poor, and when you poor, you get pulled into all kinds of mess you don't wanna be a part of.

Fooby comin into my room hidin from Crips was happenin more often lately, and that Hummer runnin up over Berno, well, let's just say I was kinda expectin it. I got a part in my own bad ways, you know. I mean, who goes around headbuttin people? I can't afford no doctor either. I'm barely able to pay Chester the rent and I'm pretty damn sure he don't give it to the woman who owns the buildin, like he pockets it for hisself. But I got a space and I got to use it.

After I kissed Mila good night, real soft, I locked the door and sat down on my bed to write out my thoughts. You lose some blood and see a friend chased down like Berno, man, it shake you up. Fooby came to hide for a minute and left real fast. My nerves was just startin to feel it. I was tired of feelin unsafe all the time. Like I didn't have the right to feel safe, but I never did.

Suddenly, I got a knock on the door and I was about to ignore it when I heard Mack C's voice. When I opened the door, tho, that drunk mothafucka was holdin two pieces of sliced yellow cheese in one hand and two harmonicas in the other.

"Baaaaaa!!!" he yelled, and fell down sideways, laughin. I helped him up and he offered me one slice of cheese and one harmonica. I ate that cheese. Then we started blowin them harmonicas and laughin and I know I was holdin back and Mack C knew it too, so he said, "Blow it!"

I couldn't play that thing but I blew, man, man, man, I blew. I blew with my friend and somehow we made somethin sound good cuz it was real. Mack C always help me find that place, bring me back to the place I forgot. He was my shorty.

After we quieted down, we sat talkin and I told Mack C to help hisself to books.

"Man, this place is like a chicken coop," he said, thumbin through *Invisible Man*, "and we be the chickens!"

"Yeah," was all I had.

"And Berno, was that some shit!? I done tole that niggah to stop fuckin them other boys' bitches. You can't fuck another niggah's bitches, I'm sorry."

"Yeah," was all I still had.

"Look, Ben, you about the whitest niggah I've ever seen or the niggahest whitey. Haaaaaa. Come on now, you know Mack C just fuckin witch you."

You couldn't hate nothin Mack C said. Cat's soul was wide open as the beautiful sky. He was right tho. I was in chicken coop in this apartment buildin, buncha cocks and hens walkin around peckin they own shit.

I didn't wanna feel helpless.

But I did.

I didn't wanna feel poor.

But I was.

I didn't want see awful shit eery day. But it was put in front of my eyes like a last meal, like a man gon die who gets that last-ass meal, like some lame-ass food gon make you forget you about to be a dead mothafucka! That last meal was some booshit.

"You streets, Ben. This here may be a buildin but it's some streets."

Mack C left after that and I was by myself again, thinkin about what I couldn't change.

CHAPTER 3
The Hoop

Now, all ya'll prolly got this idea that I'm short. But I'm six-five. Yeah. Keep readin before you got anymore jive stereotypes to lay on me. We all met at the hoop the next day, just some damn rim, no net, over in this lame-ass "park" where eerybody doin drug deals while we try to play on some asphalt that look that the highway. We might as well play *on* the highway. Prolly safer.

I looked over and who you think I saw but Kit Fisher in a green helmet tryin to do some back flips. Now that was a messed-up mofo.

The we on the court was Mack C, Crowner, Fooby and me. See, we liked Berno even tho he was a dumbass. And yes I'm usin "was" cuz he died in the ambulance last night. Berno liked pussy but he didn't know no boundaries. You got a ring on yo finger, he **gon** fuck you.

So we two-on-two and we only got half-court cuz they some tall-ass Wilt Chamberlain niggahs eyeballin us (my whiteness mostly) on the other side. Normally, we'd play, but today we had to talk about what we was gon do about Berno. This was some shit. Couldn't even see who done it from the tinted windows in the Hummer.

"I seen em," Fooby says. He on my side for two-on-two.

"You ain't seen nothin," Crowner yells back. He and Mack C on the other side.

"I seen em. And they white," Fooby says, pushin the ball up to me.

I slammed.

"Well," says Mack C, checkin the ball, passin to Crowner who shoots some nasty ass air ball (haa). "Um, Crown, please, you makin me look white. No offense, Ben. Serious, tho, ya'll realize that this is *show*down. Wild westness about to happen."

"Yeah," we three almost say together.

"Now," Mack C kept on, "I didn't like what Berno did, and I done told that idiot to do the right thing time and time again, but you fuck a man's bitch and laugh in his face cuz you doin it, you gon get shot or run over like he got done."

"So what are you sayin, Mack C?"

"I'm sayin I woulda fucked them bitches too. Haaaa. Now we need some guns."

We ended up playin them other cats across the court, and you can never have a street game without it gettin ugly. It was four-on-four, Crowner throwin elbows, Mack C stealin balls left and right and Fooby finally trippin one guy. He fell like a giant tree gettin axed, but when he looked up, there was red fire in his eyes and steam comin from his nose. Ohhh shit.

Another fight. But, see, they was trippin our asses, pushin us around the whole time, especially me. I was tall as them four Wilt Chamberlains, and they didn't like it, eyeballin me, nudgin. One mothafucka kept pinchin my ears and nipples.

Now, Mack C, Crowner and Fooby weren't tall, but they was some scrappers. And Crowner was wide. Mack C quick. Fooby sly. So Fooby trips the guy and we all waited for him to stand.

Four-on-four now, except we ain't playin no basketball.

They stared at us, we held their ugly stares.

"Ya'll calm down," I warned them.

"Who you tellin to calm down?" the knocked-down guy yelled.

"I think he was talkin to you." Mack C . "I mean, he was *lookin* at you and *pointin* at you, so who the hell else you think he means?"

Our four new enemies started walkin at us. We all shrugged a "what-the-fuck-why-not" shrug and ran at them. You talkin about a brawl.

Crowner fights like a cobra, his fists like teeth. First thing I see is Crowner crush a knee with the heel of his foot then them quick fists connectin on and crackin some faces. And Fooby was throwin the basketball right at the nuts of one of them.

Mack C was skinny and deceptive. He goes over and pulls down the sweatpants of one of them tall mothafuckas and pushes him over, kicks his ass sendin the cat hobblin away. So we was one-on-one now, pickin our duels. My duel was with the same one who'd been starin at me since I'd gotten there. He came up to me, nose-to-nose, breathin on me.

"Get yo white ass outta here before I kill you," he threatened.

"You ain't killin nothin. My momma's black by the way."

"Fuck yo momma, you white!"

Man, I had to do it. I had to headbutt his ass. I jumped up and cocked my head and came down on his nose before he could know what hit him. Blood gushed out like a water hose and he grabbed his face. But I just kept on headbuttin, kept on jumpin up and comin down and crushin his face.

I saw Mack C was in trouble and needed to finish off the one in front of me. You don't wanna have my head buttin on your ass. I was dizzy, bloody, about to pass out myself when I just pushed that giant idiot over and he fell, cryin into this hands. I ran over to Mack C and pulled the guy off him, kicked his face about thirty times and checked on my boy. Crowner had taken care of his and Fooby had crippled the knees of his. They was finishin them off with face kicks, teeth droppin onto the asphalt like rain. Mack C was in bad shape, so we needed to get him home. His mind was stronger than his fists.

Just as I wiped my eyes I looked over to the chainlink fence behind the basket and saw Mila, starin at me. She didn't run. She just held her mouth open, turned slowly and walked away.

"Mila!" I yelled.

But she was just noddin no, no, no with her back to me.

Aw naw, I said. Why she have to see *that*?

I thought maybe Crowner had killed his guy. Maybe he had. We had to get Mack C home and restin. The four of walkin down the streets of L.A., man, what a sight. We coulda been a zombie film. But we all had our teeth and we was all movin.

"I'm hurt," Mack C said, limpin. "I think I broke my leg."

"You didn't break nothin but yo titties," Fooby told him.

"I'm serious, man!"

"I wish they'd broke yo mouth!"

I don't know why we laughed. We did tho. We stopped and laughed, slappin our knees.

We was some scrappy mofos. We was gettin a name for nobody-better-fuck-with-us.

Thing about street fights: you don't go to the hospital cuz your ass ain't got insurance. And you don't have no time to recover cuz there's usually another fight the very next day.

Them fights add up tho. They was addin up for me. For all of us.

And Mack C was gettin too old. Crowner was still a cobra with his fists of sharp teeth. He was tired of it tho. I could look at him right now and see his bitter eyes. And, yeah, Fooby was young and stupid and quick, but he prolly had another fight comin up in a few hours with some Crips.

I had to find Mila and try to explain. I can't believe she had seen me doin what I did. We was like junkyard dogs out there, killin and bitin the hell outta each other for no damn reason.

Some people just hate you.

Ain't nothin you can do but fight back on that hate.

They stare you down and make you into one of them.

They make you hate cuz that's all they is.

You have to become hate to kill hate.

Don't give me no lecture about lovin my enemy and turnin the other cheek. The only cheek I'm turnin is my ass when my draws fall down and I be moonin them hatin mothafuckas! I may hate while I'm fightin cuz I have to. I have to.

Ain't got no choice when they comin right at you.

CHAPTER 4

The Snoop

Detective come around the next day axin eerybody questions about Berno. We was all limpin. Mack C was a little better, said he pissed blood all night. I worried about him. Crowner had a gash on his neck from a bite. And Fooby had gotten into another fight like I said he would. But he young. Let him fight while he can, I guess.

Now, it's funny. Berno was a pain in all-ya'll's asses, but you woulda thought he was Captain America or some shit by the way folks in the buildin was talkin about him. "Ooooooooh, Berno, we miss him sooo much, he was such a good young man."

I can't wait til I die so people start bein nice to me again!

The snoop was wearin hisself a, check it, *pink* three-piece suit with a vest, plus some hat that all the racists down South used to wear in the 50s. I could see him down the hallway talkin to crack-rock Chester and couldn't make out his face yet. Mack C, Crowner, Fooby and I were out on the stoop. Thing is, I was expectin some white racist from the looks of that hat, but Dick Cox was Japanese or some shit. When he came out on the stoop, that snoop was all nice to us. I think we relaxed when we saw he wasn't white. Colored brothas from the same motha anyway.

"I need to ask you kind gentleman a little bit about this fellow, Berno, who was killed here recently."

"Yeah he was killed," Mack C said, snortin with laughter. "They killed him so hard, he died twice."

"Where you from, niggah?" Fooby axed him.

"Why, Hawaii," he announced, proudly. "Detective Dick Cox." He tried to high-five us, leavin his hand high and dry when we kept ours in our pockets. But Fooby relented and gave him an indifferent low-five.

"Berno got what was comin," Crowner muttered.

"How so?" Detective Dick Cox responded.

Mack C: "He was fuckin around with some shit he won't supposed to be fuckin around with."

"Such as?"

"Common knowledge. He liked to ball other guys' girls."

"Did anyone see the people in the Hummer?"

"I did," Fooby said.

"And?"

"They was white. Nobody believe me. But they was."

"You're sure?" Detective Dick Cox was writin it all down on a pad.

"Yeah. They was old too. Couple of sixty-year-old guys or somethin."

"Hm."

"What?" Fooby started in on him. "You expectin me to say it was a couple of young black kids?"

"Not at all. In fact, your description fits the profile of the same Hummer running over someone up on Melrose."

"No shit?" Fooby replied. "I tole you they was white!"

"This is very helpful. Thank you. Please call me if anything else like this happens or if you're in trouble. I'm here to help."

"Yessir," we all sort of mumbled.

He was okay, the snoop.

"Now, I talked to just about everyone in your building and know you were Berno's friend. I hope you won't take matters into your own hands."

"What," said Crowner, "like trackin em down and killin em?"

"Yes, exactly not like that."

I was sure the snoop smiled tho. He knew we was capable hands.

"We ain't the killin types," Fooby informed him, his teeth spreadin wide as a jazz piano.

"I hope not."

Detective Dick Cox handed me a card and then walked down the steps of the stoop. Mack C shook his head, Crowner spit, Fooby yawned and I put the card in my front pocket. The three of them had to go do somethin, so I stayed on the stoop and tried to relax.

■ ■ ■

I had only been there a few minutes after they'd left when Mila come walkin out the front door, lookin fine, pretendin I wasn't there. I stared at her and she was shakin her ass like she knew she had one, like that ass was sayin, "Sorry, Benjamin, you done fucked up!"

Still, I ran after her and had to at least try.

When I caught up, she was on the sidewalk walkin fast.

"Mila, come on now, hold up, hold *up*."

"You bad news, Ben."

"I got some good news in me tho."

"Oh yeah? Like what?

Truth was, I didn't have none.

"That's what I thought," she said.

"You right," I admitted.

"You on a terrible path and I don't want to get close you and watch you go down it."

I just nodded and listened. You got to listen to women give they little lectures.

"I mean, I came out to the court just to watch you. I like to watch you. Then all that fightin go down."

"They came after us," I said, weakly.

"Well, learn how to walk away! Damn."

She was right. I didn't know how to walk away. I was always walkin into bad things.

I had walked into her tho and she was a good thing.

I knew the difference.

"I wanted to surprise you," she said, almost cryin now.

I leaned into her to hug her and she resisted for a second and then let me put my arms around her.

"I'm sorry, Mila," I whispered. "I'm sorry you saw me like that."

"We both in a bad place," she cried. "I hate that buildin and I shouldn't judge. I done my own bad shit."

"You wanna talk about it?"

"We all do stupid things, Ben. I ended up here cuz I done some myself."

"What?" I axed. "What did you do that was so bad?"

"I'm dealin with it. Just keep holdin me okay?"

"Okay."

"Let's hold each other more before this all gets worse."

"Okay," I repeated.

"I know what you four are up to."

"What?"

"I know you gettin some guns."

"Yeah," I said. "Berno won't perfect, but he was our friend."

"Just be careful."

"Hard to be careful with this shit."

"You come see me tonight," Mila said.

"Tonight? You sure?"

"Yeah, I'm sure."

"Okay."

"Around two a.m. Eery night you come see me and check in. I have to know you okay. Don't matter if I'm asleep. Just open the door. I'll keep it unlocked for you."

"I will."

"You promise?" she said.

"I promise."

"You better."

"You not scared of me, Mila?"

"I see you got some good in you."

"You do?"

"Yeah, I do, Ben, but I'm scared."

"You want to know the truth," I said. "I'm scared all the time."

"I know, baby. Just come see me like I told you."

"I will."

"You better. Or I'm gon kill you myself."

CHAPTER 5
The Loop

The four of us didn't have no damn money, but we was all likin the idea of gettin some guns. Crowner knew where we could buy them. Still, we had to come up with some quick cash. Fooby said there was a loop around the park where we could hit a buncha parkin lots and steal some stereos or mug some people.

"Small time," said Mack C.

"Yeah maybe," admitted Fooby, "but how about some of them ATM machines on the same loop?"

Crowner leaned forward. Mack C nodded. We was out on the stoop again.

"I seen them ATMs," Crowner said, real excited. "They just out in the middle of nothin."

Mack C: "But you can't crack them bitches open."

"We ain't gon crack open nothin," Fooby informed us. "Cuz I got an idea."

The next day we met in the park and the plan was real simple: pull four knives on some couples or women, take them to the ATM, get them to give us cash, then let them go. Didn't wanna hurt nobody.

We met right near this ATM that looked like a robot or an alien. It was just outta place. Turned out to be the right place for us. I'll flash through this scene cuz I ain't proud of it, but when you ready for revenge, well, you do what you have to do.

We decided to wear Halloween masks. I was Dracula, Fooby Frankenstein, Mack C a witch and Crowner a zombie. We was some scary shit, hoppin outta the bushes with our knives. We did it right in the middle of the day and it was hot as hell under them masks. The first couple was older and they gave us $400 just like that, runnin away as soon as they handed us the money.

Next we hit two white teenage girls who said "like" like it was goin outta style. "Like, yer, really, like *robbing* us?"

Then two gay men seemed think it was a joke. "Oh my god, the tall one, what's your name, he's hot! You, I like your length. Give him some more money!"

Not wantin to push our luck, we stopped after the fifth, counted up our loot. The couples were mos def the way to go since both of them usually had ATM cards.

Once we agreed to stop on the fifth couple, we found a place in the bushes, took off the masks and counted the money.

It was around $3,000, and nobody got hurt.

On the way out, we stuffed the masks in the bottoms of trash cans.

Thing is, we still needed another $3,000. We was only halfway there.

CHAPTER 6
The Scoop

Of course, it was in the newspaper for the next few days, and them journalists like baby maggots on horse diarrhea. But we played them. See, we knew them journalists would be up on that shit, so we just decided to use them. We had to. How they knew to come to the buildin, I don't know, but they was on the stoop the next day. It's like they *knew* we was doin it, and I had to give them props on it, but they couldn't prove it.

Then we was on the t.v. cuz there was some hidden camera around the ATM! In our masks. Man, we didn't have a lot of clothes, so you could see us wearin the same shit we was wearin all the time, plus me bein tall as a dumbass, it didn't take much to figure who it was. Didn't matter. It was vigilante on gettin back at the folks that killed Berno. Message sent.

I guess sometimes,
outside the law,
there's a right thing
the way
it supposed to be,
and when people see it,
they know it, see.

We talked to the journalists and they axed a bunch of questions, mostly things that they didn't know nothin about.

Then crazy Foob up and says, "Yeah, we did it. And we comin after whoever killed our friend Berno."

Them journalists was scratchin them pencils when they heard dat!

About then, a t.v. van rolled up and a buncha cameramen poured out. Fooby played it up too.

"Are you the Halloween Vigilantes?" this blonde, plastic-surgery-faced woman axed me with a microphone up in my face.

"Yeah," I said. "Yeah we is."

"Rumor has it that two white men in a Hummer killed him. Was this a hate crime?"

"Hate crime!" Mack C yelled. "Eery crime a hate crime!"

Fooby had his opinion about that Hummer. "I think they was aimin for Wig here, instead of Berno, but somethin went wrong."

"But," said the reporter, "Berno was black and short and Wig is tall and white. How do you explain your theory, I'm sorry, your name?"

"Fooby. Well, Wig *look* white but he black. And Berno was in the wrong place at the wrong time. That's all I'm tryin to say." Fooby seemed to be retreatin on his story.

"Naw," said Crowner, grabbin the microphone. "Berno was fuckin some white chick and he had it comin."

Fooby grabbed the mike back from Crowner. "See, my theory is that them white dudes in the Hummer knew Wig was here. He just moved here a few weeks ago. Berno been here forever and they coulda taken him out whenever, but they didn't. And Berno been fuckin white chicks since I known him. So it just don't make no sense to me. Trust me, Wig's a target. Berno was just a warnin."

"Interesting," said the reporter, noddin and grabbin back her microphone. "Thank for talking to News 6."

CHAPTER 7
The Dupe

We still needed money, and we had a plan. Chester was all crack-rock high in his studio apartment, and we knew he collected rent in cash from tenants who didn't have no credit. I knew for a fact that he had a cash stash that he was supposed to give to the buildin owner, but he usually kept most of it, and the owner was too afraid to come around to this place. I also knew he might chew through that stash if we didn't get to him before he smoked it.

After the t.v. crew left, we knew the snoop wouldn't be too far behind, axin questions, so we went straight to Chester's door, the four of us, and knocked.

It was lookin good up until that knock. I still remember that knock, thinkin we had half our money and a solid plan. The news was on our side, makin us look like heroes.

But, man, that knock messed us up.

We was waitin for Chester, but he didn't come to the door. Now we could hear his ass moanin inside like he always did, and you could smell crack smoke, hell, even see it floatin up under the door crack like a ghost. Mack C banged harder on the door.

Crowner yelled, "Yo, Chester, open up. Gots to talk to you."

Nobody thought about tryin the knob, so I did and it turned. We all looked at each other and I pushed the door open a little more. The sight would break the hardest man's heart. Chester was naked on the floor, crawlin around.

"Where's my green puppy?" he kept sayin and slobberin, and he was pullin out his afro with his hands, pullin out clumps of his hair. He was cryin too and rollin around on the floor when he won't crawlin. Like he was a baby again. Man, that crack is some shit. I done it twice and that was three times too many.

"Chester!" Mack C yelled. "What the fuck, niggah!?"

Fooby just stared at him.

"He dyin right here!" Mack C yelled. "We need to get him to the hospital."

Chester was pukin up on hisself, axin for that puppy, whatever puppy that was. You could see his piss and shit oozin over the wood floor. And if you looked a little closer, you could see some dried shit that prolly had been there for a few weeks. Man, this was some sad mothafucka about to die!

"Shut the door," I told Fooby.

Fooby closed it, tryin to be quiet.

But we was all thinkin the same thing: the money.

Crowner and I started lookin around for the cash pile.

Fooby stood by the door just starin his eyes out.

Mack C tended to Chester, tryin to slap him awake.

"You crazy niggah," Mack C said, but he couldn't be mad.

Chester was gon to die right in front of us and we was stealin from him. We just come at the wrong time.

Then I saw it. It was a stack of bills. Now Chester may have lost his mind, but he had about $10,000 stolen from the apartment owner. There were a couple of duffel bags and we stuffed them.

"We can't just leave him here!" Mack C yelled.

"Forget that crackhead," Crowner told him.

Now, Mack C, I ain't never seen him like dat. He jumped up in Crowner's face and pointed at him and they was about to go at it, when I stepped between them.

"We takin him to the hospital," Mack C informed us, barin his teeth. "And *then* we gon buy some guns. But I can't live with myself if I don't get him some help."

"Aight," Crowner relented. "But we droppin his crack-ass at the curb."

Fooby robbed a black livery cab, a Lincoln Town Car, on Wilshire and drove it up to the buildin.

We had dressed Chester in his red robe, stuffed his dazed ass into the back and put the money in the trunk. As we drove him, he wouldn't be quiet either.

"My puppy was so little."

"Shut up Chester."

"It was a green puppy."

"Man, you high."

"It was little green puppy. I miss her tummy."

I hope I never get to the point where I'm so high that I'm blabbin about some green puppy.

We drove to the hospital where Crowner and Mack C pushed Chester's ass onto the sidewalk. Luckily, there was a nurse who saw him and grabbed his hand, and that whole time he was sobbin about his puppy. Man, when a man goes down like that, it's ugly, it's sad and it's terrible. But that was all we was gon do.

It was time to buy some guns.

Now you think steppin into Chester's place was bad. Wait til you hear what happened next.

We was tryin to keep our heads clear with all the adrenalin. And all of us was happy that Chester didn't die on us. But now we needed to figure out what was next. Crowner had the connection. We counted the money and it was about $13,000. First, he handed us each $1,000.

"Whatever happens, ya'll take this so you have some walkin-around money."

"What's next?" Mack C axed.

"I got the guys. They axin for $8,000 for what we need. We show up, give em the cash and get the guns."

"What kind of guns?"

"Uzi, sawed-off, Glock .45."

"That leaves another $1,000," I said. "$1,000 for each of us, $8,000 for guns. That's $12,000."

"We gon hold it to be safe," said Crowner. "We don't spend it, we split it."

■ ■ ■

I thought we might go to some warehouse, but we pulled into Koreatown to some cat's stretch white Hummer limo! I'm like, what the fuck, broad daylight and shit. Fooby parked the car, we all got out, then stepped up into that Hummer, which was about a city-block long. I could actually stand up straight in it.

Inside, it was six Korean midgets in white tuxedos and pink bow ties, straight outta some 1980s bad prom shit.

That was some shit.

"I'm Crowner," he said, and dropped the bag of cash. "$8,000."

The midgets all talked at the same time: "You're late. $9,000."

"Fair enough," Crowner said, noddin, and pulled out the extra $1,000.

"Thanks," the six midgets said in chorus. "Take the guns and ammo you need."

A side door popped open right above liquor cabinet, and there were all kinds of guns mounted on the wall. Crowner started pickin shit, Fooby grabbed a few, Mack C got some and I did too.

One midget walked up and handed us a bag that we filled with ammunition.

"It's a done deal," the midgets said together. It was some weird shit, them talkin at the same time. I ain't never seen one Korean midget, much less *six*.

"Yeah," agreed Crowner, "we done. Almost."

Crowner inspected the arms, tossed us the guns he chose and had us load up. The midgets all watched. And sure enough, just as I was thinkin, hm, what idiots let a gun deal go down like this, Crowner pointed his uzi at the midgets and shot eery last one of them, just mowed them down!! Before Mack C, Fooby and I could catch our breath, he walked over to the money and grabbed it back.

"Wig," he yelled to me, "drive this mothafucka. We got an upgrade."

And we got the fuck out with the money and the guns.

I took it slow, pullin out and drivin west down Wilshire.

Crowner had flipped out right in front of us. "Take this onto the highway," he said. "Get on the 10 goin to Santa Monica."

Fooby and Mack C were speechless lookin at them six dead and bloody midgets in the back of the Hummer.

I found the onramp to 10 west and next thing I know, I hear Crowner axin for help. He had rolled down all the windows. I looked in the rearview to see him and Fooby pickin up them midgets, one by one, and tossin they asses out onto the highway!!!!!

Mack C still speechless.

I stared at the side mirror and saw a midget hit the highway and splatter, cars crushin the body.

All six bodies were tossed out the windows.

"Keep drivin, Wig!" Crowner shouted. "We almost done back here."

When the last midget was out, I watched all the cars behind me screechin and slidin, as the final body landed on the windshield of a red Camaro. Cars pilin up all over the damn place.

"Take the next exit!"

I veered off.

"Where to, Crown?!"

"Take a left then go about a mile. I'll tell you where to stop."

I kept drivin and Mack C came up to sit with me in the passenger seat. He was just shakin his head. "I ain't never seen no shit like that."

"Yeah," I said.

"We in deep now."

"I know."

Crowner and Fooby came up to the front with us.

"Now, listen to me," Crowner started. "That was some ugly shit, but that was also some personal payback I had to take care of. They framed me before I went to jail cuz I ain't no wife-beater. I brought somethin personal to this, but I knew what I was doin and I'm glad none of ya'll got hurt. So listen up. We gon hide this Hummer and now we got some cash we gon need. I didn't wanna buy no guns and end up with nothin again. I'm tired of nothin."

He guided me into what looked like an old factory. I rolled down my window. I pulled the Hummer to where Crowner told me, and about twenty Latinos appeared from nowhere, whistlin cuz they was impressed.

"Eerybody out," Crowner said.

We had our guns and money, and we was waitin. The Hummer disappeared and what reappeared in our trade was four cars, one each. We couldn't afford to be fancy, so they was real basic. One was a Dodge Omni, one a Ford Pinto, one a Chevy Chevette, and one a Jeep. But they was all suped! Them Latinos can take a cheapass car and make that shit beautiful. They disappeared with the Hummer almost as fast as they had appeared.

Crowner took the Jeep, I took the Chevette, Fooby the Pinto, Mack C the Omni. We packed our guns and our share of the money in each car, so nobody had it all. Then we had a little talk.

"Now Fooby," Crowner said, "what makes you so sure about these dudes who took down Berno?"

"I ain't sure about nothin. I just saw what I saw."

"Well, we need a plan. We got it all in place, but we ain't got no damn plan. I done my part and got the guns and cash. But pretty soon that snoop gon be findin some dead midgets on the highway, so we got to act fast."

We hadn't thought it through, he was right. All we had was two white men in a Hummer. And our dead friend, Berno, who wasn't really that great of a friend.

"See," Crowner said, "I ain't doubtin you, Foob, but you was real confident with that t.v. reporter wif all yo theories, which makes me think you holdin back on us."

Fooby looked nervous.

"You hidin somethin, Fooby?" I axed.

Fooby looked at me. He sighed. "Yeah, but ain't like you think."

"What's it like then?" Crowner said, inchin closer to him.

Mack C was still shaken up and had gotten real quiet.

I watched Fooby and Crowner and was hopin nothin bad would happen.

"Like I said," Fooby insisted, "it ain't that way."

"You better talk to us," Crowner said. "If it ain't like that, then you ain't got nothin to worry about."

"Aight," Fooby relented. "It's like this. Wig ain't gon like it."

"What's this have to do with me?"

"It's yo dad, Wig."

"My dad!?"

"Yeah, that's who was in the Hummer that killed Berno. I don't know the other guy. But I know the driver was your father."

Crowner grabbed Fooby's arm. "How you know!"

"Don't want to talk about it."

Fooby yanked his arm away.

"What happened?" I said. "You have to tell us."

"Yo daddy been snoopin around the buildin for a few weeks and finally I seen him go into Chester's crib. Berno and I seen him so we figured he was bringin Chester his crack and shit. I didn't know it was yo dad at first."

"How did you find out?"

"Berno was payin his rent and smokin some crack with Chester. I wasn't smokin but I was with em in Chester's raggedy-ass place. There was a knock and this white dude come in axin for you, for Wig, sayin he was yo dad and shit."

"Ain't this a bitch!" Crowner muttered.

"Well, Berno start talkin shit and they got into a fistfight, but yo dad was high on somethin cuz he was actin outta his mind. He kept sayin he was goin to slaughter you, Wig, which is why I told the t.v. woman that I think somethin went wrong. Yo dad high as a mothafucka. Prolly got pissed at Berno and wanted to mow him down, but I'm pretty sure he was hopin you were on that stoop too, Wig."

"Makes sense," I admitted.

I looked Fooby in the eyes. He won't lyin.

My own father comin after me.

He always been comin after me.

I was an accident he hated and it was my own whiteness I saw, not my father.

"Shit," said Crowner. "I'm sorry, Wig. I mean, Ben."

"And," Fooby added, "turns out he been supplyin Chester with that nasty crack. Prolly fucked himself up in the process."

"Yeah," I said, "he was doin that shit when I was a boy."

"The man ain't seein straight," said Fooby. "I'm real sorry I didn't speak up, but I didn't think it would get this bad."

"Thanks for tellin me," I said.

"You still in?" Crowner axed. "I mean, this yo *father* and shit."

"I'm still in. We takin him down."

"You sure?" Mack C finally spoke.

"He's comin after me either way."

You can only kill
hate with hate.
Love too late.

"We need to go," Crowner told us, lookin at his watch.

"I think I know where he might be," said Fooby. "Not positive, but we can try there first."

"We'll follow you."

"Keep yo guns ready cuz he's got some backup."

"Showdown," Mack C said. "I'm some John Henry Doc Holliday shit today."

"About time you woke up," Crowner said, punchin Mack C's arm.

"That midget killin kinda got to me. Phew-wee!"

"Ha ha," Crowner said. "Yeah, that won't right."

In a line of cars we followed Fooby.

As I drove I was kinda hypnotized by it all, my body sore, my mind filled with too much, too much, man. I kept shakin my head hopin the thoughts would fly outta my mind.

CHAPTER 8
The Whoop

Fooby lurked around in the night and could find just about any place, and he was right on the money.

I knew cuz we drove right up to my father's house, the very house I'd been kicked out of.

"You can't kill your father," I kept sayin to myself.

What was we doin?

It felt like things was happenin and we was just a part of them, like we couldn't control the flow, we was just flowin.

My dad's house was by itself in the middle of nowhere. He had been hidin for a long time, buildin up his guns, thinkin eery urban legend was true, eery conspiracy theory was actually happenin. I would come down to the basement and he'd be watchin some nasty porn and smokin his crack pipe, meltin his mind and fillin up the leftover part with stupid shit.

I say I was kicked out, but I left as much I got the boot.

None of it surprised me.

My dad just wasn't all there in the head.

I just never believed I'd have this kinda of showdown with my own father, tho. Maybe it was meant to be like this.

Our cars pulled up about a half-mile away from the house, and we walked with our guns and ammo. Not the brightest idea, but he was out on 100 acres and no one would see us. It was dark by now anyway.

He wanted to be alone, well, he'd be alone when it was his time.

The four of us walked down the road like we was goin to Tombstone.

"I ain't mean to scare ya'll," Fooby said, cockin his gun. "But he got about thirty men up in there."

"Thirty!" Crowner yelled.

"Yeah, I seen em when I came out here once. I got curious. Yo daddy connected to some kinda bad."

"We doin this?" Mack C axed. "I mean we really doin this!?"

"Yeah, Doc Holliday," Crowner said, "too late to stop doin it."

"We can stop," I said.

"Nah, we ain't stoppin," said Fooby. "We doin what needs to be done."

We walked on in the night, our steps echoin, them guns gettin heavy in our hands, extra ammo on our backs.

It wasn't a far walk. Felt far tho.

We came to the long driveway and figured we'd just walk down it.

None of us had much to live for.

We didn't care about dyin.

They couldn't see us until we got to the house cuz my daddy was too cheap to buy video cameras for the property.

We were in the yard but in the distance.

Fooby was right.

There were armed men eerywhere. And I know he didn't pay them much.

What the hell had my father turned into?

The more I heard, the less I was surprised cuz I guess we all saw it comin.

"Fuck it," I said. "Let's go."

We charged at those men, no thought about it, and we had the guns and we shot and shot and men just kept fallin, men in suits, all white men, and since we caught them by surprise, we mowed them, all of them.

They won't expectin us. We'd scoped out a tree each to reload and came out strong again.

Hell, we won't expectin to do it either, but when you was beat up as we was, and you had nobody, you didn't care.

I thought of Mila, yeah, I did.

And I was just stupid, yeah, shit I knew it.

Maybe it was that simple: I was stupid. I didn't know better.

But, see, I *did* know better and I still did stupid shit.

I was killin more people in a few days than most murderers.

So is that what I was?

Or was I better than this?

All these thoughts crammed my head as I laid rounds into that trash.

It was suddenly silent.

The men in the yard were dead.

And Mack C was dyin too.

I leaned down to him.

"Shit Mack."

"Wig, I don't give a fuuuuck."

"Love you boy."

"Love you boy. Go!"

He died as I stood and stormed the house, Crowner and Fooby right behind me.

Fooby was shot in the hand. Young. He good.

Crowner was okay.

I was shot through my ear. All good.

Inside the house, I was a boy again. This had been my home.

Crowner walked ahead of me. "I *got* this," he whispered.

I knew my dad was in here.

I felt him.

He felt me.

The street was some fucked-up killin fields and all they did was lead me right back to where I came from.

When we found my dad, it was nothin like I had expected.

It was nothin but sad.

He looked like a skeleton, his face was whiter than ever, his body bony. He was smokin a rock and I thought, man, that's it, he ain't even gon come after me?

We would only find this out in the comin days, but my dad had been sellin crack all over the city. In fact, he was known as the biggest seller of it. Chester had been buyin from him, and eery fucked-up crackhead had somethin to do with my father. I couldn't believe it.

His sins were my sins, but I wasn't gon inherit him anymore.

On top of that, he needed to be put out of his misery, like some sad horse that has lived way past when it should have.

Only, have you ever tried to shoot a horse?

A horse is beautiful, even an old one.

A father is beautiful, even a damaged one.

But there I was.

I saw my father before me. And I started to feel that it was time for me to live right.

Crowner had my back.

Fooby had my back.

Mack C was dead.

Mila was waitin.

I didn't have to die, but he had to.

"Nah, I can't," I said. "I can't do it."

My father looked up. "Just please do it, son. Let it be you, not one of these useless city niggers."

Now, you may think we got all mad after hearin him say dat, but we laughed our asses off! We was hoppin around just laughin cuz, shit, my father was no father of mine. He never had been.

He wanted to die.

We all wanted him to die.

He'd had a hard life. People called him wigger too. Called him white trash. I could almost see the kid he was and how he came to be at this place right now.

If had been a Christian, I woulda forgiven him, loved him, picked him up, saved him.

I wasn't a Christian.

I was one of the Halloween Vigilantes.

I was Wiggah.

I was Benjamin, yeah.

But I was mostly Wiggah.

Wig for short.

I was makin peace with myself, as my father spoke again.

"I'm sorry I said that," he said, talkin to Fooby and Crowner.

Fooby looked at me. I looked at Crowner.

"I'm real sorry," Dad said. "I need to watch my mouth."

"I can't kill you," I told him.

"You mean . . . you'll let me live?"

"I said *I* can't kill you. That's why Fooby gon cap you."

Fooby stepped forward. "I owe you, Wig, for a lotta shit, but we even now."

"Cap him," I said. "We even."

Fooby capped him.

I ain't feel nothin.

Well, that ain't true.

I felt good. I felt okay.

I felt like I got rid of a real bad part of myself.

I watched death come into my father and life go out of him.

As he died, he kept apologizin so I know there was a good man in there. Somewhere, once.

Now, I know my ex-daddy had some cash stashed too and we found it. I knew exactly where it was. And we split the rest eye-to-eye even. We had all the money from the ATM and the midgets, and with my dad's nickel, it turned out to be about $100,000 each. I didn't feel right takin a bigger share just cuz he was my dad. My boys had fought for me, and I give back to those who got my back, you know?

CHAPTER 9

Shoop Shoop

Well, Mila was left and I had to repair it. My body and head was all mixed up in her, twistin me back to that girl. I went straight to the buildin with my money and my guns cuz, yes, you need yo guns these days, but I tossed mine in a trash can a few blocks away after I thought about it, went into the buildin straight up the stairs, and I just opened her unlocked door.

And you want to know some timin shit?

It was two a.m. just like she told me.

I cracked open the door, my bag of money on my shoulder. I heard her stir. "Ben?"

"Yeah. It's me."

"Mmm, you lived?"

"Ha ha, yeah, I lived."

"You ready to come to bed with me?"

"I'm ready, yeah, finally ready."

"You figure it all out?"

"We lost Mack C."

"I'm sorry. Come here."

I walked to her bed and dropped the money, just poured it out all over her like champagne.

She didn't even turn on the lights. Didn't *need* to.

"Now, it ain't a lot," I told her, "but it's a start."

"Oh it's a *good* start." She was smellin that money in the dark.

But then she just pushed it all off and grabbed me and I fell into her, and I ain't stopped fallin since.

Of course we buried Mack C, buried his ass with a real funeral too, and you know what? Chester even came. It was me, Crowner, Fooby and Chester. But we laid him in the ground proper, Mack C. My boy. He liked to read. I said a few words about how he would borrow books from me and how he had a family he loved. If there still was a Doc Holliday today, it was Mack C. And in the end Mack C had fought for me.

Later, we got Chester in rehab with some of the money, enough for two years for him to heal. He got off the junk, so we felt good about that. Now he writes poetry about puppies and apparently they are makin some damn movie out of it. Some poetry puppy movie. I ain't kiddin.

Fooby, man, I thought he might burn through his money, but he didn't. I mean, he did the whole stripper, limo, pimp thing, but the kid was smarter than I thought. He come up to me a week later and gave it back, told me to invest it and help him. So I did. Except, he had managed to spend $20,000 in a week. That's fine. I got the rest back cuz I saw he wanted to be smart.

Crowner, damn, *got* to prop him up. He led us right! Goddamn bulldog. But bulldogs are more intelligent than you think.

See, after all that crazy killin, we separated. After about a week, tho, we knew we was connected. So Crowner comes up to me, I'm up with Mila and he axs if I want to be partners.

"What kind?"

"Damn Wig, I don't know. But partners. I kinda miss yo ass. Ain't nobody like you. You a fighter like me, but you don't want to fight. I respect that. I wish I could find a way to stop fightin."

I told him what happened to Fooby, how he spent some of his money but came around.

"You know what," I said.

"What?"

"I got a plan."

My father didn't have no will, so the house went to me after a few wrangles with some judges and lawyers. When I informed them about their teenage daughters and the crack addictions and love of black dick, they moved my case through real fast. Funny how some black dick can oil the wheels of justice.

Momma had killed herself a long time ago. I can't even talk to that cuz it makes my heart sad.

After Mack C's funeral, we had to get out of that damn apartment buildin.

All at once we moved out, just left, except my books. I brought my books with me.

We had my dad's big house and I let Fooby and Crowner live there.

They let me handle the cash and I paid them salaries to be "bodyguards" which was some booshit, but they liked it cuz they didn't want to deal with the money.

When Mila saw the house, she started in on changin it. She wanted to make it ours. And she gave it her touch.

The snoop came around to the house one day in his same pink suit. I thought he was comin for trouble, but he nodded with appreciation. He even axed us if we had any work for him. He became our friend. Never axed us about the midgets. He was from Hawaii but somehow became our boy. I even started payin him. Fooby and Crowner called him Higgah cuz he was our Hawaiian niggah.

There it was: Fooby and Crowner with Dick Cox, the pink-suited detective on our side.

I was protected.

And I got Mila.

We had dinner eery night, me and Mila, Fooby, Crowner and Dick.

We was the good guys.
We was alright.
I was home again and I had held my ground.
Won't nobody scarin me off from myself anymore.
Watch out for the streets cuz sometimes they run right up into your home, no matter what your home is.
That shit had all worked out tho.
I had found the good in me.
Sometimes, that shit just works out.

COMING SOON

JULY 2012

Mark Damon Puckett's
THE KILLER DETECTIVE NOVELIST

A schizophrenic detective, Mack Harris, befriends a novelist across the hall in his apartment building in Manhattan. After a series of supposed deaths, Mack has to figure out why his reality has been so subverted. In this writer's labyrinth, Mack begins to develop an actual life outside the character he is in the book. And the question becomes: who is in control here, character or novelist?

THE KILLER DETECTIVE NOVELIST

The Relief of Death

He had a weak spot for the dead, some kinship with quiet bodies. It put the silence in him, made him quieter. He felt complicity with death, lauding its terminatory potency, a giant hand slapping down human flies, crushing so many with one swat.

He did not like the dying.

And he did not like the living.

It was with death itself only that he had this affinity, attraction even. He loved death. He desired it. He couldn't wait to die himself.

If death were a person, it would be his nightly drinking friend.

Being alone, that is, loneliness, was a particularly different mortality, a daily repetition of feeling alien on alive sidewalks, a governor of nothing. And sometimes he was such a stranger, so saliently dead-but-walking, that when he finally happened upon another death, finding a dead body, that is, it was as if his recognition of the dead merged with his own dead self, and in some odd negation, he grew comfortable, never repulsed.

Only death brought him back to living.

This body on the floor (how many deaths this week?) was so frail that lumps of bone pressed under her skin.

Mack Harris stared down at her face.

Feminine, he thought, even with the vomit on her neck.

He grimaced and let out a breath, but he still had to run his index finger across the bile and taste it, knowing that he would retch.

You had to touch the dead, he thought. His gagging surged, was suppressed. You had to touch people even when they had died because they probably just had not been touched enough when they were living. This was the essence of all the current irritability steaming from everyone's noses, being untouched, living by neighbors and never inviting them into your house, snarling at faces simply because, deep down, you only wanted to talk to them.

She had fallen from her bed and lay sprawled on her back. A constellation of red, white and yellow pills were dotted on the floor around her bleeding head, reddened blue eyes orbiting in the blood. The red and the white and the yellow and were so bright that they glowed, but the red of the pills was different from the red of the blood. Real blood was brown.

Sadness rushed up from in him; it had started as nausea but changed into to something simpler. What began inside never came out as what it had been. The grief, first in his stomach, emerged only as water around his eyes.

How was this?

How did things that were once so strong weaken into other things?

Grief for the dead; it changed itself all the time. Grief was perfect when it started, distorted when it finished. He could only conclude that what trueness of pain originated in a person was perfect, for a second at least, and then it became the wrong version, nothing like it was, a simulacrum of what had originally made it grand.

Inside is grander, he thought. *My outside is not real.*

Rage, a thick needle in a small vein, punctured him because of these contradictions. He had no way of reconciling what was in with what was out and thought of John 20:17 to calm his mind. "Noli me tangere," a resurrected Jesus warns Mary Magdalene. "Keep your hands off me."

Was Christ angry for being alive again?

To have been dead and forced to live again seemed the worst doom. And was he hungry, having not eaten while he was dead? Did this esurience give Christ a hollow stomach and make him irritable? Was this same hunger the reason he was aggravated with Mary Magdalene?

Mack knew why Christ did not want to be touched, for he was still dead in his own thoughts. To be touched by Mary would mean acknowledging life. To not be touched would allow him to remain in the posture of death. Christ's limen, therefore, was an impossible threshold, for he was alive but just formerly dead, and the only way he could remain in this nexus was by simply using semi-threatening language to a woman who loved him.

Don't touch me.

One thing was clear: Christ loved death more than life.

Mack held the grand in him like Christ's liminal place. Christ had known actual death. And when he lived again, he had the memory of death. Mack held each death he saw within him, and these memories were not unlike what Christ had done after he had re-lived.

It was a resistance, certainly, this fixation on death as better than life.

What was inside him was not necessarily privacy as most people saw it.

It was also not sacred, which was a terrible, misused word.

It was internal.

Leave the inside of me alone.

There were no perfect words for the internal. How could you create words for what was impossible to define, one's immanence? Definitions were traps, words pretending to articulate ideas but only capturing them in the end. God, naming God, was the worst reduction of all.

Follow me, Mack said to himself.

Just follow my head.

I am making sense.

I see *it*, sense.

I see sense.

Why then does nothing come out as what is should be?

The best people were the ones who knew the maze of language.

The novelist!

He had to find the novelist.

He loved the novelist and his writing lightning.

Mack was just like the writer. Only he, Mack, could not express himself.

The writer could.

In his head, yes.

Out of his head, no.

This is why he needed the novelist.

He also knew that the novelist plagiarized his insanity.

Which was fine. Since Mack couldn't do it himself, he was glad someone else could.

The novelist gave him money from the stories he wrote about Mack. There had been at least two books.

Yes, the novelist had stolen from him, in some eyes.

In Mack's (eyes), he had expressed what was only locked in his own head.

The novelist was a vulture who came at the right time. Weren't vultures gorgeous, though, on the side of the road, eating death as if it was a normal dinner?

You had to admire vultures.

Serious birds.

Many would say the novelist was bad for Mack; he (the novelist) was not, however, because he gave Mack what he required. Mack needed for someone to know about what he thought; it was important.

Also, the novelist calmed him because he *listened* to Mack, just sat there and heard him. When those books were out, Mack read and reveled in them, mostly because the novelist had conveyed it correctly! Had this writer listened listened so well, or was the old novelist prone to his own darkness too?

Hmm.

Mack kind of loved the novelist.

The novelist was poor and yet spent all his time around stories. All he cared about were stories. He was terribly unhealthy, eating mostly blue cheese and pretzels and smoking Lucky Strikes or red Pall Malls.

What was the novelist's name?

He couldn't remember.

The novelist would give Mack money and have no food for himself, so Mack would buy food and give it back to him. Why did the novelist do that? He had some kind of creed, stealing Mack's stories but giving him money, even when he (the novelist) had no food.

So they shared many meals, drinks, drugs, even cheese together.

Yes, the novelist was all right.

He *tried*. Tried to remain aware while also being an outsider.

ISBN: 9780983543503
Author: Mark Damon Puckett
Publisher: Onion Scribe Publishing
Learn more at:
www.markdamonpuckett.com

"*The Reclusives* by Mark Damon Puckett had me laughing out loud, in public places. Every story is unique insight into the beauty of our internal thoughts as individuals living in a very externally driven world. The stories acknowledge a shallowness that exists in people and our way of living everyday conversation . . . but the way they acknowledge it, is by great depth. Provocative, puzzling, and bizarre, but always honest and vivid. It moves like we move."

—CRITIC ERIN BOYLAN

". . . . a very worthwhile experience, especially for those drawn to the accessibly avant-garde."

—CLAYTON LACHMUND,
author of *The Innocence*

"With *The Reclusives*, Mark Puckett has written a gem of a collection. Each story is what a writer might scrawl on the backs of rejection letters for submissions that followed the rules set by workshops and literary journals. The language is impatient and emphatic, stating directly those first associations of image and meaning that come from the creation of narrative made of the observed absurdity of daily life. Freer and more open to asymmetric logic than the typical short story, each reflects the psychology of their protagonists, who, while recluses, are not rejects. Rather Puckett's characters are recluses from the hypocrisy of the cliches that construct the go-nowhere 9-to-5 work-a-day world. Their inability to remain tidily numbed by the sedative of no-meaning makes them unable to just be. A salary man discovers the cubicles of his office have the internal logic of a multi-floor crossword puzzle. A novelist finds success only by writing unpublishable novels in the voice of a Czech literary figure who does not exist. A Willy Lomanesque businessman has his moment of self discovery in the halls of a dog show among artificially coiffed poodles. And in the extended final piece, 'Pool Man', Puckett lets rip an ecstatic freebase of an odyssey with twist after twist through an absurdist but eminently logical landscape that folds one moment upon the next. All the while, Puckett manages to maintain a sweet regard for his 'reclusives', allowing each character the opportunity within their story to achieve a certain uneasy peace with themselves, their positions in this whacked out world, and move on into whatever awaits them beyond. The results are frequently curious, never quite what is expected and always very smart. I can heartily recommend his work to those for whom the status quo feels a bit more like a strait-jacket. This is a good book and one worth taking for a swim."

—POET JORN AKE,
author of *Asleep in the Lightning Fields*,
The Circle Line and *Boys Whistling Like Canaries*

"In these nine stories Mark Damon Puckett doesn't just run the gamut, he runs laps, caroming from character to character and a variety of experiences, with each tale leaving an indelible mark. A wonderful collection."

—NOVELIST JEFF GOMEZ,
author of *Our Noise, Geniuses of Crack*
and *Attempted Chemistry*

"Impeccable. This is simply a great read! Too often, short stories are so driven by theme that they fail to pull the reader in through the characters. As a writer of novels and a reader who likes to be pushed and pulled on an emotional level as well as an intellectual one, I found Mark Damon Puckett's collection a pleasure. The writing is exceptional, but where *The Reclusives* truly shines is within its quirky and haphazard assortment of human beings. This book will make you think and feel and laugh out loud as you see myriad parts of yourself, and everyone you've ever met, come to life. These are stories that will stay with you long after the book has been read."

—NOVELIST WENDY WALKER,
author of *Four Wives* and *Social Lives*

"Just tore through *The Reclusives*, simply because it is one of the easiest tomes I've read in a long time! The characters are so compelling, so accurate—I *know* these people, man! These are real people. Reclusive? Yes. Neurotic, you bet. A cross-section of the underworld ethos of a misanthropic, neophytic, awkwardly social generation. And I raise my glass to them and celebrate each of them! For without *them*, who are *we*?! I truly enjoyed it. I laughed out loud, and I empathized. Great characters, and wonderfully delicate stories."

—TODD DUFFEY,
Actor, *Office Space* and *Buffy the Vampire Slayer*

"Puckett's characters invite themselves into your consciousness and then start rearranging the furniture. You're never quite sure who let them in, but once inside, they're there to stay. They're odd, damaged creatures, these people—somehow both ingratiating and rude at the same time—in other words, strange as they are, they're real."

—DAVID THOMPSON,
London Critic

www.ingramcontent.com/pod-product-compliance
Lightning Source LLC
Chambersburg PA
CBHW050141110726
47898CB00008B/2614